"You may dress like a man, but that doesn't mean you can defend yourself like one. Why are you traipsing around like you stole some trapper's clothes off the line anyway? Did no one ever teach you how to behave like a lady?"

She sucked in a breath sharp enough to rival an offended church lady. With no thought at all, she hooked her ankle around the major's legs and toppled him to the ground in a most unladylike fashion. In hindsight, she knew she never would have accomplished it if he'd been expecting an attack. Before he could get up, she placed a booted foot on his shoulder and leveraged herself up onto his horse's saddle. She prayed the beast was merely misunderstood and not actually dangerous as she jerked the reins from the major's hands. A brief glance confirmed he'd already rolled away and was rising to his feet.

She made a clicking sound. "Yah!" Demon took off like a shot. Estelle looked over her shoulder at a dusty, fuming Major Tucker.

Too Wyld for Comfort

by

Shelley White

Wylder West Series

Too Wyld for Comfort

Cover Art by *The Wild Rose Press, Inc.*

The Wild Rose Press, Inc.
PO Box 708
Adams Basin, NY 14410-0708
Visit us at www.thewildrosepress.com

Publishing History
First Edition, 2023
Trade Paperback ISBN 978-1-5092-4944-2
Digital ISBN 978-1-5092-4945-9

Wylder West Series
Published in the United States of America

Dedication

To John, my very own sexy man in uniform.

Chapter 1

Wylder, Wyoming November 1878

Estelle jumped onto the platform before the train came to a complete stop. She needed to find Wabli before he found trouble or trouble found him. He didn't understand the world was nothing like *Horton's Wild West Show* where they both grew up. She didn't know much outside of show life either, but she did know that Indians—even half-breeds—weren't welcome in many places unless folks bought tickets to see them there.

She passed two passenger cars before the train finally squealed to a halt with a hiss of steam. Porters already had half the baggage car unloaded by the time she reached it. She took note of her saddle amongst the trunks and bags but left it for the time being. No one would steal it; it was far too distinctive. Besides, no self-respecting cowboy would be caught on a saddle boasting so many useless flourishes. She wouldn't herself but for the fact she owned it outright, a bequest from her mother. Estelle didn't like it, but she treasured it because Gilda had loved it.

Another porter unlocked the stock car. Restless animals pawed the wooden floor inside. Estelle noticed the chill around her for the first time when the door slid open, and she was buffeted by the smell of warm manure and straw laden air. Her palomino, Starlight, fairly

1

glowed in the dim light of the car. She clicked her tongue and Starlight settled and whickered back. The porter stepped inside, and Estelle followed holding up her claim ticket. "The palomino." She pointed at her horse and the porter unlatched Star's enclosure.

She greeted her friend and clipped a lead rope to the bridle. The porter placed a small ramp and she and Star followed him onto the platform. Since no one came forward to claim the car's other occupant, a tired-looking red mare, the porter moved to the next livestock car only to hesitate.

As folks collected their belongings, several gravitated to the car carrying nothing short of a ruckus. The horse inside was letting all and sundry know it was not at all pleased with its situation. The car shook, and the door rattled with what sounded like a forceful kick. The horse inside screamed its displeasure. The porter tucked the key in his pocket and returned to the first car. Estelle didn't blame him.

Retrieving her saddle and bag, she settled one on Star's back and the other on her shoulder. *Now where?*

A woman with a tight gray bun and pinched expression bustled toward a trio of women standing on the platform looking lost. "Ma'am?" Estelle touched the woman's sleeve.

The woman stopped mid-stride and turned to stare at Estelle. As her gaze dropped from Estelle's faded hat to her fringed leather coat, canvas trousers, and finally to her battered boots, her face pinched impossibly tighter. She inhaled through her nose but didn't respond.

Estelle decided she'd better get her question out before the woman walked off. "Can you direct me to the livery?" She used her best manners, gleaned from the variety of actresses she'd known in her life.

The woman glanced at the three women on the platform, then back at Estelle. "Go east on the road that runs along the tracks. It's the last building on the way out of town. You'll smell it before you see it." She sniffed. "Or maybe you won't."

The slight rolled off Estelle's shoulders, it being nothing she hadn't heard before. She may look worn, but she wasn't unclean. She tipped her hat. "Thank you, ma'am. Have a fine day."

She led Starlight down a ramp to the dirt street. *Is there anything in this town besides saloons?* There were two directly across from the train station waiting to whet the thirst of weary travelers. A couple of men in uniform staggered out of one set of batwing doors and headed west toward a building labeled Cavalry Office. She'd never heard of the cavalry having space outside of posts or forts. But that wasn't her world. Her world consisted of performing Indians, painted ladies, sharp shooters, and crowds, always crowds waiting to experience the real wild west. She patted her coat pocket, reassured by the small lump created by Flora, her double-shot Derringer.

She nudged Star and they set out eastward, maneuvering around wagons waiting to pick up arriving travelers. Only one other building beyond the rail office fit the location the woman gave. The attached corral in back proved she'd found the right place.

Star's ears perked and she let out a whinny. Her pace picked up and Estelle struggled to keep up.

"Slow down, girl. I know you want to stretch your legs. I'm sure there's grain there but try to act like a lady."

An answering neigh split the air and Star would have broken into a trot if Estelle hadn't been holding tight. She focused on the corral and found the object of Star's obsession. Thunder, her brother's blue roan, paced and stomped at the fence.

Estelle allowed Star to lead her there rather than the front of the building, her original destination. If Thunder was here, Wabli must be too.

The pair met at the fence and nuzzled in greeting. Estelle scratched behind Thunder's ears then gave Star equal attention lest she get jealous. "Where's Wabli, hmm?"

"You know this horse?" A grizzled older man stepped into the corral leading another horse. He unclipped its lead and smacked it on the flank, sending it trotting to the far side of the enclosure.

"Yes, he's my brother's horse."

"Welp, you send him on over to claim him and pay up his keep." The man pulled a faded bandana from his pocket and wiped his nose.

Estelle frowned. "My brother didn't board him here?"

"Nope. Stolen. Got a fella locked up waiting on the circuit judge to come through." He stuffed the soiled cloth in his back pocket.

What in tarnation? Her pulse spiked in worry for her brother. He and Thunder were inseparable. "This is Thunder. I'll pay his keep, and I need to board Starlight as well."

"Might fine. I'll meet you 'round front." He ambled back to the barn.

She pulled Star's lead. "Come on. You'll be reunited soon enough." *Then I'm going to the sheriff's office to get some answers.*

Chapter 2

Ft. Laramie, Wyoming

Farewell, Company K. Major James Montgomery Tucker hammered the final nail through the lid on his crate of personal belongings. This parcel would ship straight to Boston. He'd have no need of his bullseye lantern, sorely outdated plaid sack coat and trousers, nor his packet of certificates and accommodations during his brief assignment in Wylder.

Wylder, Wyoming, a town barely bigger than Fort Laramie, yet an important cog in the distribution of men and supplies to surrounding Forts Laramie, Collins, Russell, and Sanders. A cog Tucker needed to unstick before he could start his life as a civilian and never have to lay eyes on the frontier's endless prairie ever again.

Tucker planned to take leave enroute and spend time with his sister in Chicago. Those plans dissipated when his colonel handed him orders and a train ticket and told him to fix the problem. Wylder's sheriff wired the fort with some serious complaints about the cavalry office there. Serious enough that Tucker carried with him a letter of authority to demote and/or detain Captain Edward Dooley. Seemed Dooley stepped on some toes in addition to poorly managing troops while they were under his command.

He packed a satchel with his remaining belongings:

his second uniform, small clothes, shaving kit, Bible, .45 colt, and ammunition. He scanned the shelves for missed items, his gaze landing on a small bisque doll. The European-made frozen Charlotte doll stared at him accusingly, always accusingly, with dull black eyes from her spot on the shelf. Her woven blanket and beaded hide cradle preserved her modesty as she leveled Tucker with her unwavering glare.

Tucker shook his head. Even as he longed to leave Indian territory behind, Charlotte, his talisman, would be joining him in Boston. He hated the doll and cherished it in the same breath. She was a reminder that man, under the noblest of causes, will perform unspeakable acts. She reminded him of his own humanity and that separating from the cavalry was the only way he could prevent it from slipping away for good.

He placed the doll in his satchel between the clothing so she wouldn't be damaged and buckled the bag closed. Whatever Wylder had in store, he knew it wouldn't be burning teepees, ransacking villages, or dealing with Indians.

With nothing left to do but collect his horse, Demon, from the stable, he took one last look around the barracks that had been his home for the past two years. He wouldn't miss it. His parents, his home, and his law career waited for him in the East. The West and all its inhabitants could rot in hell.

****

"'Bout time someone showed up." With a hint of a wince, Wylder's sheriff rose from his desk.

Tucker stepped forward to shake the older man's hand, preventing him having to walk too far on legs clearly paining him. "Major James Tucker, sir. I was sent as soon as could be arranged.

"Earl Hanson, Sheriff, if it ain't obvious. Have a seat." The sheriff settled back into his wooden chair.

A glance out the front window confirmed Demon still rested, tied securely to the rail. Originally, Tucker questioned the point of spending ninety miles in the saddle only to take the train for the final thirty. The ability to get a bath and change into fresh clothes at a Cheyenne hotel warmed him to the plan. He arrived in Wylder rested and cleaner than he would have been otherwise. Demon adamantly disagreed.

Upon retrieving the half-wild stallion from his private livestock car, he met with sour looks from the porter and other passengers alike. Leaving his bag on the platform, he wrestled a saddle onto the beast's back and rode him hard down the road leading out of town. When the fight settled out of him, he pointed him back to town and the sheriff's office. There was no one he trusted more to have his back in battle, but he feared the horse wouldn't conform to civilian life as easily as his master.

As a result, Tucker's crisp, clean uniform wrinkled, and he could feel a band of gritty dust under his collar. Not how he'd intended to present himself as a representative of the United States Cavalry. He sat in one of the two wooden chairs across from Sheriff Hanson's desk. "Your wire was urgent but vague. We want to maintain good relations with local law enforcement. If you'll tell me your concerns, I'll do everything within my power to address them."

Earl snorted. "Concerns." His chair creaked as he leaned back. "Over the years, I've turned a blind eye to the goings on over in that corner of town. So long as your deadbeats and no accounts kept to their own and didn't bother the good citizens of Wylder. I'll retire eventually, and I'll be damned if I leave that nonsense to my replacement. There's been an uptick in soldiers passing through gettin' their last hoorahs at the saloons and the Social Club. Miz Adelaide's complained, as have several other legitimate business owners on that end of town. At least one lady's been harassed by your men."

Tucker frowned. "Sounds like deportment protocols need to be readdressed with the leadership here."

Earl snorted again. "That's not even the worst of it." He leaned forward in his chair. "Your man arrested a kid in my town. My town! Arrested him, locked him up in his office, and contacted the circuit judge." His face was red now as he jabbed his finger into his desktop.

"Excuse me?" Tucker leaned forward as well. "The US Cavalry has no jurisdiction here. What happened?"

"This kid—"

"First, define kid. Are you saying he detained a child?"

Another snort. "Kid about seventeen, mindin' his own business. I wouldn't have looked twice at him. He weren't breakin' no laws. Your man accused him of horse thievin' an' had him locked up before I even arrived on the scene."

"Was the horse stolen? Is the boy a local?"

"Claims the horse is his. No one else has come to claim it. Kid had been in town 'bout a day. Made the mistake of ridin' past one of the saloons. Couple of recruits took issue with him and hauled him to your Captain who agreed the kid was up to no good and locked him up." Earl opened his desk drawer and pulled out a pipe. He stuck it in his mouth but didn't light it, then slammed the drawer shut.

"Is the horse particularly valuable?" The story wasn't adding up in Tucker's mind.

"Blue roan gelding. Indian pony, by the looks of it. Well trained, for what it's worth."

"What made my captain not believe the boy?"

Tucker turned as the front door opened. A figure stepped through and shut the door hard enough to make the glass panes rattle. Sheriff Hanson jumped to his feet and Tucker followed suit a hair's breadth later.

"I want to talk to the man who stole my brother's horse," the figure, who turned out to be an oddly dressed woman, demanded.

The sheriff tipped his hat and moved out from behind his desk. "Ma'am, that's not precisely how things are done 'round here. Why don't you come have a seat and we'll discuss your situation?"

She huffed and walked farther into the office. Tucker moved to the side, allowing her his chair. She stared at it but made no move to sit, forcing the men to remain standing.

Earl addressed Tucker. "Major, if you'll allow me a moment, I suspect your two problems may be connected."

Tucker didn't miss the sheriff's reference to *his* problem, as if it were no longer Earl's problem. Tidy, that. He nodded in acquiescence.

"I'm Sheriff Hanson. Who might I be addressin'?"

The woman, if she could rightly be called such in her canvas trousers and deerskin coat, glanced at the empty jail cells, then narrowed her eyes at the sheriff. "Hanson. Are you a doctor, too?"

"Nope. You're a might young to know of him, but my late pa used to be the doc in these parts. You need medical assistance?" His gaze flickered over her body.

Tucker took the opportunity to scrutinize her more closely. Her clothes were shapeless enough that she might be mistaken for a man from behind if not for the blonde braid hanging down her back like a thick golden rope. She'd removed her hat and more gilt wisps floated around her sun-bronzed face. Freckles covered her forehead, nose, and cheeks. He'd never known a woman to be so careless of her complexion. His mother and sisters would take to their rooms for a week if a single brown spot dared take up residence on their pampered faces.

"There's nothing wrong with me. Why isn't the horse thief locked up?" She planted her hands on her hips.

Tucker answered. "There's a person detained at the cavalry office. I've just arrived in town to handle the situation, as it was my captain who apprehended the suspect. Before you walked in, I asked the sheriff what evidence there was in the case."

They both turned to Earl.

"Sit down, the both of you." The sheriff lowered himself into his seat. The pipe, which he'd set on the desk when the woman entered, he stuffed back in the desk drawer. He pointed at her. "Now you. Who in tarnation are you, and where and who is your brother?"

And why in the world are you dressed like that? Tucker wanted to add, but her attire didn't seem to faze the sheriff one bit.

She sat on the edge of her chair with her back as straight as any finishing schoolgirl. "My name is Estelle Adleton. My brother ran off a week ago. I know he was heading here, and I came to find him. I found his horse

11

at the livery and Mr. Daniels told me it was stolen. That means my brother is missing and may be in trouble. I need to talk to that horse thief."

"What's your brother's name? We get new folks through Wylder pretty often." Earl opened another drawer and pulled out a pencil and pad of paper.

"Wabli Horace Adleton Cetanwakuwa. Shall I spell it?" She rose out of her seat a bit.

Earl laid down his pencil. "Ah, mmm. No need." He turned to Tucker. "You asked 'bout evidence against your horse thief. The only evidence your captain thought he needed was the fact that the kid he arrested was Indian. Now I'm no judge, and I don't wear no fancy uniform, but I suspect a walk over to your cavalry office will clear up a bit of this problem and find Miss Adleton's missing brother to boot." He looked back at Estelle. "How old's your brother?"

"He's seventeen. What's going on? An Indian stole Wabli's horse?" She stood, knocking her chair back with her calves.

Earl ignored her question and rose to his feet, too. "He your full brother, or is he part Indian?"

Estelle sniffed and tipped her chin up. "He is my full brother in all ways that count."

The sheriff raised one eyebrow and met her gaze.

She sighed. "We have the same mother. Wabli's father is Lakota Sioux."

He responded with a nod and turned to Tucker, who had also risen. "Now here's the problem. Circuit Judge is already on his way. You can go to your office and release Miss Adleton's brother, if indeed that's who's locked up. But if the judge arrives and there's no case to try, he's bound to get a bit tetchy at us for wastin' his time." Earl held up a hand before Tucker could interrupt. "Regardless of who was responsible for the wastin'. He's liable to haul everyone in front of him to hear the case anyway and come to a contrary ruling just to spite ya. Judges don't tend to like folks takin' the law into their own hands."

Tucker smiled. "That seems an unlikely scenario."

Earl shrugged. "How long you been in the west, Yank? And I mean the real west, not your fancy fort or chasing Indians off their land?"

Estelle cut in. "I don't want to leave my brother in jail!"

Earl's gaze softened, and there may have been a slight smile beneath his mustache. "Missy, your brother's in a locked room with all the creature comforts and three squares. I've checked on him several times myself. Other than being a bit scared, he's safe. He's read through half the books on the shelf in his room and I know his mattress is more comfortable than the hay in the livery where he slept his first night in Wylder. I'm sure it'll be a comfort for him to know you're here."

He eyed Tucker again. "I'll admit I've got my own selfish reasons for wantin' to maintain the situation until the judge gets here. I've been fussin' at your captain for the past two years to straighten hisself out and get his men in line. I'm thinkin' maybe he'll listen a might better to a court appointed judge who'll have no truck with an overteppin' captain. In fact, that's a sure way to guarantee the case gets thrown out."

"I'm here to assess the situation and report back to my superiors. At this time, it seems there's a strong case for reassignment." Tucker had hoped this stopover would be quickly managed. Now it looked like he'd be waiting for the judge.

"I'd like to have seen him gone two years ago. He's out of line and high on authority. He's calling for a hangin'." He glanced back at Estelle who'd paled considerably. "When we're done here, I'll point you to the attorney's office here in town."

"I'm an attorney. I'll handle it," Tucker said quickly.

"Conflict of interest, but I don't imagine it matters much in this case. You gonna escort Miss Adleton?" He tipped his head in Estelle's direction. She'd gone quiet and seemed to be processing the information.

"I will." Tucker put out his hand. "I apologize for the trouble the cavalry office has caused in town."

Earl shrugged and accepted his hand. "Not all bad. Make up about thirty percent of the saloon's business and the same, if not more, at the social club. They just need leadership who'll make 'em mind their manners a bit."

Tucker eased Estelle toward the door.

She allowed it for a moment, then stopped and turned back to the sheriff. "Wait! Can you tell me where to find Millie Lowery?"

Earl blinked. "Mrs. Mildred Lowery?"

"Yes. She's er, a distant relation." Estelle glanced around the room, making Tucker suspect subterfuge.

He scratched his head. "Huh. If the major'll take you west on Wylder Street, you'll see Sidewinder Lane past the Vincent and before the mercantile. Lowery's dress shop is just after the corner."

"Thank you and thank you for keeping an eye on Wabli. I don't know that I agree with keeping him there, but I can't make any decisions until I speak with him." She offered her hand as Tucker had.

Earl stared at it before grasping it awkwardly and giving it a half shake. "A pleasure, ma'am. Good luck."

Chapter 3

"Don't touch me." Estelle shook the major's guiding hand from her elbow. Once outside, she stopped and gazed at the street and buildings around her, trying to get her bearings. She'd walked from the livery, taking a side street that spit her out just west of the sheriff's office. The hotel and mercantile were in the opposite direction. She could probably find Lowery's Dress Shop on her own, but the cavalry office must be on another street.

"Come. I'll walk you there." The major stepped off the boards and walked to where a beautiful, dark bay stallion stood tied to the rail.

"It'll be quicker if we ride." She followed him and raised a hand for the horse to smell.

He quickly maneuvered in front of her, blocking the motion. "That's not a good idea. Demon's in a bit of a temper about his rail accommodations. He's liable to bite your fingers off."

Estelle rose to her toes to look over the major's shoulder. She stood almost six feet herself, but the man before her topped her by at least five inches and his chest seemed twice as broad. The horse's ears swiveled, and he butted his head into the major's back, sending him forward into Estelle.

He grasped her shoulders to keep them both from toppling. "See. He's ornery."

She shrugged off his grasp again. "I know my way

around horses. I need to see my brother so I can figure out what we're going to do." She tried moving around his solid body.

The major frowned while easily blocking her again. "There's nothing for you to figure out. Dealing with the captain in charge is my responsibility and that also makes your brother's welfare my responsibility. The sheriff knows the judge, and I'm satisfied to follow his suggested course of action."

She stepped to the side, and he mirrored her motion. "Listen, there's things you don't know. It would really be best to just release Wabli, since it's been established he didn't do anything, and let us skedaddle on our way."

He narrowed his impossibly blue eyes at her. "Why don't you tell me what I don't know? Are you two in trouble with the law somewhere else?"

"Of course not! It's none of your business."

"You're not going to tell me what I don't know, and it's none of my business if you're in trouble with the law?" He folded his arms in front of him as if he didn't even need them to keep her away from the horse.

Estelle stomped a foot. "Argh! Our family business is none of your business, and we are *not* runnin' from the law. Now let me by."

"Ah, I see. You're running from your family." He smirked. Before she could respond, he turned and untied his horse. "We'll walk. I can't even trust Demon not to throw me after the day we've had." He held the horse on his right and offered her his left arm.

She spared it a glance, then forged ahead, taking a right out of the dooryard, hoping it was the correct direction. The major sighed, but didn't stop her, and quickly caught up on his longer legs. He didn't offer his arm again, which was a relief. She didn't like men touching her.

"Is this your first time in Wylder?" Was he nosey or making polite conversation?

"Obviously."

"Not really. You asked about Lowery's. Do you have friends or family here?"

Nosey, Estelle decided. "That falls under the category of not your business." She kept her eyes pointed straight ahead.

"I only ask because we've just passed Sidewinder Lane, and I would point it out to you. But I see you're in a hurry to get to your brother. I can escort you back later."

She turned her head to see people coming in and out of the mercantile. At least she'd easily remember the landmark. "There's no need. I can find my way back." She took note of the hotel on her right as they rounded the corner onto Buckboard Alley.

"The days are getting shorter. I won't let you walk back in the dark. I've not been to Wylder for a couple years, but no town is safe for a lady to wander around at night."

Estelle rounded on her escort and poked a finger in his chest. "You don't know anything about me. I am more capable of taking care of myself than most men."

"You may dress like a man, but that doesn't mean you can defend yourself like one. Why are you traipsing around like you stole some trapper's clothes off the line anyway? Did no one ever teach you how to behave like a lady?"

She sucked in a breath sharp enough to rival an offended church lady. With no thought at all, she hooked her ankle around the major's legs and toppled him to the ground in a most unladylike fashion. In hindsight, she knew she never would have accomplished it if he'd been expecting an attack. Before he could get up, she placed a booted foot on his shoulder and leveraged herself up onto his horse's saddle. She prayed the beast was merely misunderstood and not actually dangerous as she jerked the reins from the major's hands. A brief glance confirmed he'd already rolled away and was rising to his feet.

She made a clicking sound. "Yah!" Demon took off like a shot. Estelle looked over her shoulder at a dusty, fuming Major Tucker. Up ahead, she saw the train tracks through a gap between the buildings. *Ah, the town is simply a rectangle.* She recalled seeing the cavalry office earlier when she'd left the train station.

She pulled back on the reins, and the horse completely ignored her. She didn't panic, but bits of her conversation with the major popped into her mind like the first drops of rain before a deluge. This was the horse in the livestock car causing a ruckus. Her vast experience with horses came from working with well-trained show, trick, and stunt horses, not unruly war horses.

The cavalry office whipped by, or rather she whipped by the building. She leaned to the left as they careened around the corner to Cheyenne Road. *Perfect. They could lock her up for horse thieving next to Wabli.* Folks jumped out of the way as they came through and Demon dodged a cart full of barrels.

Old Cheyenne Road led out of town. She needed to change direction before Demon set his sights on freedom. A side street came into view past the Longhorn Saloon. Yanking hard on the reins, she forced her ride's trajectory to the left. The sharp turn caused Demon to slow. Estelle fought with him as he tried to return to the main street.

She would have none of it. "Listen here, you. I know you're capable of better behavior than this. You're sore at the major; don't take it out on me. Now let's go pick up your boss before we both get in trouble. I won't tell him you were goin' for broke, but you gotta take the blame for runnin' off in the first place."

Demon's sides heaved as he took her scolding, responding with a snort.

"Yeah, well, I know he won't believe it, but you've known him longer. I may have use for him later, so I gotta' make nice." She also needed to control her temper better. "Do we have an understanding?"

Demon pawed the ground and snorted again. They'd begun to draw a bit of a crowd. By her estimation, the alley to her left should take them back to Buckboard Alley and hopefully be less crowded. Keeping Demon at a sedate walk, they made their way between the buildings. *At least I've found Lowery's Dress Shop.* She glanced to her right but continued on.

As they emerged from the alley, a dusty and disgruntled major stopped his trudging and waited for them to approach.

"I stand corrected. You appear able to brawl and ride as well as a man. Congratulations. Now get off my horse." His expression invited no argument.

Estelle slipped out of the saddle and landed lightly on her feet. She handed the major Demon's reins, contrite and, surprisingly, embarrassed. She made her living behaving similarly for crowds of people. Why did it bother her for this man to think her unwomanly?

The major checked Demon for injuries and whispered something to him Estelle couldn't make out. Probably more scolding. He then resumed his trek toward the cavalry office. She fell in step beside him. As she opened her mouth to apologize, he spoke.

"I don't think we've been properly introduced. I know you're Estelle Adleton, here from somewhere you won't talk about for a reason you won't say to find your brother who happens to be detained by my captain at the cavalry office. Does that about sum it up?"

She nodded.

"I'm Major James Tucker, formerly of Company K, Second Cavalry at Fort Laramie, completing my last orders here in Wylder before I separate from service and return home. My orders seem to intersect with your reasons for being here. You can call me Major, James, or just Tucker since you're a civilian, but you'll hear everyone else call me Major, Major Tucker, or sir."

He held up a hand when she started to interrupt. "I'd appreciate it if you would keep quiet when we arrive at the office. I'd like to hear my captain's version of events before you jump in demanding to see your brother. Please allow him to dig his own hole before I share that I've already been briefed by the sheriff. I'm not expected so I don't know what we'll encounter. Tell me you can control yourself to that extent at least."

Estelle's cheeks warmed at the mild rebuke. She deserved worse. She wanted to see Wabli but didn't want her presence during Tucker's initial interview to jeopardize her brother's case. "I can stay outside with Demon."

Tucker gave her a side eye. "There are stables. They're part of the warehouse. If you can tuck that braid up in your hat and not draw attention to yourself, you can give Demon a brush down as punishment for your little stunt."

They'd reached the office and he led her past it to the warehouse. She paused to coil her hair on top of her head like a beehive and replaced her hat, pulling the brim low on her forehead. A uniformed man leaned next to the entrance; his brim pulled similarly. He emitted a growly snore.

"On your feet, man!" Tucker yelled, causing both Estelle and the man to jump. "A party of Indians could have crept by here and set the place ablaze and you wouldn't have known till your own clothes were on fire."

The soldier fumbled to attention and glancing at the rank on Tucker's shoulder, snapped a salute. "Sir, yes, sir! Sorry Major, sir!"

"What's your name, soldier?" Tucker demanded.

"Corporal Eli Dugger, transferring from Fort Russel to Fort Sanders, sir!"

"I'm not impressed, Corporal, not impressed at all. How long till you're relieved?"

The man remained rigid with his gaze fixed ahead. "Guard changes at four o'clock, sir!"

"I suggest you do your best to impress me until then."

His tone sent shivers up Estelle's spine.

"Sir, yes, sir!" the corporal replied.

"This person is going to take care of my horse while I speak with your captain. Leave them alone. Demon is temperamental. No one else needs to be in there either."

"Yes, sir!"

Tucker led Demon and Estelle into the dim warehouse and put the horse in a stall. Crates and barrels were stacked at the opposite end of the building. Dust motes floated in the meager sunbeam allowed by a slatted window near the roof peak.

"Don't leave this building and don't take your hat off. I'll come for you as soon as I find out what's happening in the office. You and Demon seem to have established a rapport." He leveled a glare at her. "He shouldn't give you any trouble. He tends to know just how far he can push without the risk of being sold for glue."

She ignored his authoritative tone. She'd do what she wanted and go where she wanted whenever she felt like it. It just so happened she felt a little remorseful about her recent horse borrowing that she decided to care for the unruly steed. "Shall I untack him?"

"Yes. He's in for the night." Demon snorted behind him. Tucker turned and grasped Demon's bridle, bringing his head down to eye level. He spoke in low tones. "I'll not tolerate any more of that nonsense from you. If the lady had been hurt, you'd have a one-way ticket to the glue factory. Am I clear?"

Estelle may have been mistaken, but she'd swear Demon rolled his eyes at his master. He rubbed a cheek against Tucker's head, knocking his hat askew. She fought back a grin.

He stepped out of the stall and latched the door. "Keep your head down. If you have any questions, save them till I return."

"I won't have any. The sooner you get on about your business, the sooner I can see my brother." She slipped past him and unlatched the door. She greeted the horse softly, watching the major out of the corner of her eye.

He opened his mouth as if to speak, then closed it, turned on his heel, and stalked out of the warehouse.

Chapter 4

Tucker brushed at the sleeve of his wool sack coat to rid himself of any remaining evidence of dusty boot print on the navy-blue fabric. It satisfied him to note Corporal Dugger remained at attention outside the door. If that typified the kind of loose ship Captain Dooley ran, he feared setting things aright in Wylder would take far longer than anticipated.

He strode to the front of the cavalry office and entered without knocking. A man with captain insignia on his shoulder sat tipped back in a chair with his booted feet propped on the desk. Captain Dooley, Tucker presumed. The man's facial hair, sorely out of regs, needed a trim. His coat lay unbuttoned and open, and the shirt underneath untucked and stained. He fiddled with the lock action of a rifle resting on his lap.

Another man stood across from him, paused in the act of pouring a caramel-colored liquid into a scotch glass. This man, a private, at least dressed properly. At Tucker's appearance, he set both bottle and glass down and snapped to attention, flashing a terrified glance at Dooley.

Dooley looked up when Tucker closed the door sharply. His eyes flitted to Tucker's rank insignia, and he set the rifle on his desk and dropped legs, his and the chair's, to the floor. He leisurely rose to his feet and rendered a lazy salute. "Major, to what do I owe the pleasure?" Turning to the other man, he said, "Kid, pour the major a drink while you're refilling mine."

"Yes, sir," the kid mumbled, hesitantly dropping his salute.

"Don't bother, Private. Officers don't imbibe when they're on duty. You're dismissed to return to quarters."

Dooley bristled at either the edict or the dismissal of his lackey. Tucker didn't know which and didn't particularly care. This man was an embarrassment to the uniform.

"Sir, yes, sir!" The private snapped another salute, then eased past Tucker and out the door, slamming it behind him in his haste.

Apparently realizing this was not a social call, Dooley buttoned his coat over his filthy shirt. "What brings you by, Major?" he repeated with a new edge to his tone.

Tucker outranked the captain by one level, but that and the orders he carried from the Colonel held all the weight he needed to ruin the other officer's day. Ruining this man's day would likely lighten his own foul mood.

Estelle Adleton confused him. Never would he have expected her to accost him and steal his horse. Her audacity surprised him as much as her ability. He found her interesting and enjoyed poking at her, but his comment about her clothing was unforgivably rude. His mother raised him better than that. It didn't excuse Miss Adleton's behavior. He'd not let his guard down around her again.

When she'd removed her hat and coiled her braid around her head, his mouth went dry. He imagined it, loose and wavy, around her shoulders like a golden fleece. His reaction aggravated him. He wanted to stuff her in a proper dress and set her in a parlor. But he couldn't. He couldn't even punish her appropriately for stealing his horse. Fortunately, he had the deserving Captain Dooley on which to take out his frustration.

Tucker removed his hat and hung it on a peg by the door. "Numerous complaints about this office have made their way to Fort Laramie and Colonel Egar." He pinned the captain with a steady gaze and waited for the digging to begin.

The man shifted on his feet. "I'm sure that's an exaggeration, Major. If you've got some green boys complaining about the way I do business, it's only cause they ain't been in service long enough to know how things run. You know how them new recruits is." He smirked and rolled his eyes for emphasis.

"The complaints came from the town, actually. The Colonel thought they were serious enough to warrant sending me here instead of back to Boston."

The captain shifted again and tugged at his collar. "Pfft. Nothing but cowpokes and miners. We're good for this town, bring lots of money. Just ask the business owners."

"I don't need to ask the business owners. The complaints came directly from the sheriff who was speaking for himself as well as several business owners." He crossed his arms without dropping his glare.

"If the man can't do his job, he has no room to talk. He complained about that damn injun, didn't he?"

"No. He wired about gross abuse of authority, miscarriage of justice, and flagrant disregard of jurisdiction. Not to mention numerous accounts of behavior unbecoming of U.S. Cavalrymen."

The captain's face turned crimson, and he blustered.

"Absurd! The man needs to retire. He's as feebleminded as I've ever seen."

"Hm. Sheriff Hansen seemed sharp-witted for someone in their dotage. Regardless, Colonel Egan thought the complaints warranted investigation and possibly an audit of the facility." Not a task he relished as every nook in the pigeonhole shelf behind the desk was stuffed with rolled paper and a tray overflowed with more on top.

Dooley followed Tucker's gaze and cleared his throat. "I assure you everything's in order. There've been a lot of transfers lately and I haven't assigned anyone to bind last month's paperwork, or September's, neither."

"Go pack." Tucker issued the order, knowing it would be misinterpreted.

"What? Now see here, you have no authority—"

"See here, *Major*," Tucker corrected.

The captain blinked. "What?"

"Or, *see here, sir*, will also suffice. As for authority, I have a letter from Colonel Egan giving my full authority in this matter. I am now the highest-ranking officer at this facility. Since you are using the second room as a jail cell, that leaves one private room available. Go pack your things and move out to the barracks with the men."

Dooley set to sputtering.

"Take the rest of the day off, Captain. I'll settle in and begin looking things over this evening. I'm sure by tomorrow I'll have some questions or, lacking that, I'll have new duties to assign you while I'm here doing your job. I'm going to check on my horse. Be gone before I return." Tucker turned on his heel, retrieved his hat, and exited the office, resisting the urge to look at the captain's surely enraged expression.

Though curious about Estelle's brother, Tucker decided their first meeting should be in the presence of his sister. Anything to endear him and help repair his, undoubtedly, tarnished impression of the U.S. Cavalry. He didn't know the boy's background, what with Estelle being so tight-lipped, and didn't want to add to his fear.

As he rounded the building, he deliberately slowed his pace. It wouldn't do to appear anxious about his horse, or about the unorthodox beauty grooming him. The corporal snapped a salute as Tucker passed, which he didn't bother to return. As he approached, he could hear Estelle whispering to his damned horse. He would swear it sounded like sweet nothings, but surely not, not to a stallion called Demon.

She ran the brush down Demon's back all the way to his flanks. The horse shivered in delight.

A spasm chased up Tucker's own spine as if he'd felt the bristly caress as well. That wouldn't do. "Are you almost finished?" He'd hoped to startle her and metaphorically wrestle back the upper hand he'd conceded.

Estelle didn't flinch. "About." She gave Demon a few more strokes before setting the brush on a shelf. "Who's a handsome boy?" She rubbed the horse's nose and neck and he playfully knock her hat off in response. "Rotten blighter," she responded with a grin.

"Blighter?" Tucker raised an eyebrow. "Colorful vocabulary you have, Miss Adleton." He picked up her hat and offered it to her as she walked out of Demon's stall.

She flicked a hooded glance in his direction, then proceeded to recoil her hair before accepting the hat. "I work—used to work with a variety of people from all over the world."

"Work with the mysterious family you're running from?" He closed the stall and gave Demon a rub on the nose. The horse nipped at his fingers.

"Of a sort. I'd like to see my brother now." Her steady gold gaze followed him as he picked up his saddle bag and draped it over his shoulder.

"Let's fix this first." Tucker stepped into her space and used his fingers to shove an escaped section of braid back into her hat. It felt like silk. He suspected it would, and never should have given in to the temptation to touch it. He cleared his throat and moved back. "The corporal is a bit more alert than when we arrived. Keep to my left as we leave."

Her chin jutted out. "Are you taking me to see Wabli?"

"Yes." He wiped his hand on his jacket to erase the feel of her hair.

"All right." She took a step and stopped abruptly, causing Tucker to stumble into her back. He grasped her arm to steady himself. She shook him off as soon as he regained his balance. "How long are you going to hide that I'm a woman?"

"Just tonight. Come tomorrow in daylight and you should be safe enough."

She looked at him over her shoulder. "I thought I proved I can be safe on my own at any time."

"Perhaps so. By the time you finish visiting with your brother, it will dusk. I'll escort you to Lowery's." He held up a hand to forestall her response. "Think of it as saving me the trouble of having to write up paperwork on any soldier who may attempt to accost you. It's been an interminably long day."

Her eyes raked over his face. "All right."

"Let's go, then."

Chapter 5

Estelle wiped her hands on her trousers. Wabli wouldn't care, but she wished she didn't look so grungy and travel worn. Major Tucker didn't look any less crisp despite his mishap with her boot. Military grade fabrics were a miracle. "Have you seen him? How does he look?" She asked when they were beyond the corporal's hearing.

"I thought it best to wait for you. I cleared out the office, so we'd have some privacy to discuss his case."

"You were serious about that, about being a lawyer?" She stopped. He touched her elbow, glancing at the street traffic. She brushed him off and continued to the door under the cavalry office sign.

"I am. I read the law, apprenticed, and stood for exams a couple years before taking on my commission. I've served in that compacity for Company K and plan to open an office in Boston as soon as my assignment here in Wylder is finished." He opened the door and ushered her in.

She glanced around the empty office while the major removed his hat and hung it on a peg by the door. She expected something a little tidier. Papers littered every surface, and she spotted several dirty glasses on desk, shelves, and windowsills.

Tucker stepped past her and down a short hall. He glanced through an open doorway and grimaced before turning back to her. "He's in here." He nodded at a closed door opposite the open one. "Why don't you come let him know you're here." He reached for a ring of keys hanging on the wall.

Estelle took off her hat and ducked under his arm pressing her nose close to the jamb. "Wabli? It's Stella. Are you all right?"

"Stella!" Her brother's muffled voice came from behind the door. "Why'd ya follow me? He's for sure gonna come now."

She hoped the major wasn't paying too close attention to her conversation. "Don't worry about that now. Of course, I came after you. You knew I was planning to head this way soon. I just hurried up my plans a bit."

"I left clues to make him think I went to Chicago."

Estelle rolled her eyes. "I'm no C. Auguste Dupin, but your clues were flimsy at best."

"I wasn't trying to fool you," grumbled the voice.

"If you hadn't spent years begging mother for stories about Wylder and the animal talker you might've fooled him. He'll be here before long."

Wabli snorted. "Not after me."

"After us both."

Tucker stood closer to her than she liked, and she flinched when his hand brushed her side. "I need to unlock the door."

****

Tucker stood back as the boy, young man if truth be told, launched himself at his sister. The youth wrapped his arms around Estelle and tucked her head under his chin. She wasn't a short woman and Tucker estimated the kid to be closer to his own six-foot five height. He cleared his throat.

Wabli straightened and shoved Estelle behind his thin frame. He had the stature of a man, but his lack of bulk identified him as a teen. The next thing Tucker noticed was Wabli's unusual golden eye color, matching Estelle's. Nothing else marked them as siblings.

He glanced over the boy's shoulder into the room turned jail cell. A pallet and thin blanket lay on the floor. The only furniture was a wooden chair and small table. Narrow boards nailed high on the walls circled the room and served as bookshelves. Many of the tomes Tucker recognized as dry regulation manuals; new ones were issued each year. There were also a few law and history books as well as several works of fiction and poetry volumes. A book by Edgar Allen Poe lay on the table with a bit of fabric marking a spot in the middle. It seemed Estelle and her brother were well read despite their rough appearance. It also explained her earlier Dupin reference.

"Who are you?" Wabli demanded.

"Wabli, stop it. He's going to help us." Estelle deftly stepped around her brother.

His eyes narrowed. "He's one of them."

Tucker offered his hand. "I'm Major James Tucker. Please don't lump me together with the likes of Captain Dooley."

The boy ignored Tucker's hand. "I didn't do what they say. Thunder is my horse." He turned to Estelle. "Have you seen him? Is he safe?"

"He's much happier now that Starlight has joined him at the livery. I paid his keep. He's safe for now."

"Your sister has identified your horse and the sheriff said you hadn't caused any trouble in town prior to the captain apprehending you. As soon as the circuit judge arrives, there shouldn't be any trouble releasing you."

"Why can't you let me go on the sheriff's say so?" He turned to Estelle. "We need to get out of town."

Tucker frowned. He couldn't help overhearing their previous discussion through the door. Wabli seemed to have a stronger sense of apprehension about whatever the pair ran from. As a half-Indian boy who rode through an unfamiliar town bold as you please, Tucker guessed the boy's fear was on behalf of his sister rather than himself. The question was, why?

"There are complications, Little Eagle." Estelle reached up and tucked a lock of hair behind her brother's ear. Most of his shiny black locks were tied back in a tail, the only concession to the boy's heritage. Otherwise, his dress was that of any other farm boy rambling around town: dusty laced boots, too-short trousers, button-up shirt, and suspenders. A fringed trapper's coat like Estelle's hung on a nail in the wall of the improvised cell.

Wabli shook off her attentions and turned a glare toward Tucker. "What kind of complications?"

"The circuit judge is already on his way. If he arrives and there's no case to try, it's liable to put all our skins in jeopardy." Tucker explained.

"So, I have to stay in jail to keep you out of trouble? That's not very much incentive. You know I could've broken out of here at any time?" Despite the kid's bravado, Tucker didn't think it would've been quite as easy as that.

Estelle placed a hand on her brother's arm. "Wabli, stop it. It's to keep you out of more trouble."

"I can let you go. But do you really want to worry about a posse as well as whatever you both are already

Shelley White

running from?"

Wabli dropped his gaze, then glanced at his sister. "Where are you staying?"

Tucker took that as compliance. It would probably be the closest thing to cooperation he'd get from the kid.

"I'm going to look in on Aunt Millie. If she doesn't have room for me, I'll find a boarding house or bunk with Starlight for tonight."

"Over my dead body."

The siblings turned.

Tucker frowned. "If Mrs. Lowery can't take you in, I'll give you my room here for tonight. You'll not stay at the livery."

"I saw a boarding house on the way here. Culpepper's? Or the hotel." She gave him a defiant look.

"I can't recommend Culpepper's. She most assuredly won't have a room for you anyway." Tucker had had minimal dealings in the past with Culpepper's and its proprietress, but it was enough to know Estelle wouldn't be welcome.

"Then the hotel." She jutted her chin in emphasis.

"I'll escort you to the dress shop and see what happens. We can discuss your accommodations further should the need arise." Tucker really didn't want to argue with her in front of her brother. He needed the boy to trust him and work with him if he was going to serve as his counselor. Though, he'd be happy to argue with Estelle another time and place. He'd never met a woman so willing to contradict him. *Why do I look forward to sparring with her again?*

There was a knock on the door and a boy of about twelve entered before Tucker could respond. "They's outta cobbler today so Jake sent cookies for you an th'

36

pris—hey, where's the cap'n?"

"I'm supposed to get cobbler?" Wabli asked, his eyes homing in on the basket.

The boy's eyes grew wide as he jerked his gaze from Tucker to Wabli. "Is that th' pris'ner? He's escapin'!" He tossed the basket aside and scrambled back toward the door.

Wabli jumped over the desk and dove for the basket, catching it before it turned over. Tucker couldn't help but be impressed by the Indian's agility as he rounded the desk and struck his leg on the corner. He bit back a curse and nabbed the younger boy's arm before he could get out the door.

"Stop!"

The boy froze.

Tucker sighed and resisted the urge to rub at the sore spot above his knee. "I'm Major Tucker, taking over for Captain Dooley. The prisoner has *not* escaped. What's your business here?"

He looked from Tucker to Wabli, who still sat on the floor cradling the basket. "The cap'n gives me one cent a day to deliver meals for him and th' pris'ner."

"I see. Is it two of the same meal?"

"Yep, er, yes, sir. The cap'n just ordered bread for the pris'ner but sheriff Hansen said it had to be two the same an' the city is payn' for the pris'ner's meal."

"Fascinating," Tucker mumbled, raking his hand through his hair. The gruff sheriff conveniently left out that information, but Tucker was glad someone had been looking out for Wabli's interests.

Wabli looked up from peeking in the basket. "Did you say this usually has cobbler in it?"

The boy whipped his head back to Wabli as he

inched toward the door. "Every evenin' 'cept today."

Tucker sighed again. He switched his hand holding the boy, freeing his right and using it to search his pocket. He pulled out a three-cent piece. "What's your name?"

The boy's eye lit on the coin in Tucker's fingers. "Cecil, sir."

"I thank you for bringing the food and for the information, Cecil. Here's three cents for your trouble. See you in the morning." Tucker would let Wabli eat both meals. It sounded like Dooley had been short-changing him his desserts. The smell of chicken reached his nose and his mouth watered.

"Yes, sir." Cecil snatched the coin and flew out the door.

Tucker followed and drew the door shut. Dusk had well and truly fallen, typical for the time of year. Though not yet five o'clock, small towns tended to close up early as the days grew short. He needed to get Estelle settled.

"Wabli, I need to get your sister to Lowery's. Can I trust you to stay here?" He met the boy's gaze when his head jerked up.

"You don't think I'd run?"

"I think your sister is important to you, and you don't want to upset her after what she's already been through. I think you're a smart enough lad to know I won't be gone long enough for you to get very far." Tucker raised an eyebrow, daring Wabli to disagree.

He glanced at Estelle who pursed her lips, undoubtedly at being discussed as if she wasn't present. "I'll stay."

"I'll need you to stay in your room in case anyone wanders in. You can have my dinner."

Wabli's frown lessened a bit. "Yes, sir." He turned to Estelle. "Will you be all right?"

She leaned in so their foreheads touched, and she ran her hand down his hair. "I'll be just fine. I'm sure Aunt Millie will be happy to see me. I'll bring her to meet you later. You stay here and stay out of trouble. For all his pomp and nonsense, I think the major is on our side."

"Thank you for the glowing recommendation," Tucker deadpanned. "Let's go." He didn't touch her, but he wanted to. He stifled the impulse and stuffed it away, something to examine another time, or never.

"Goodbye, Little Eagle. I'll come see you tomorrow." She leaned back and turned to the door.

"Goodnight, Stella. Be safe." Wabli clutched his basket and went into his room, shutting the door behind him.

Stella looked up at Tucker and spoke in a low voice. "Will *he* be safe?"

Chapter 6

"I'll lock the door to keep anyone from wandering in. Captain Dooley has a key, but his pride won't allow him to come back tonight. He's most likely already at one of the saloons. I won't be gone long." Tucker started to offer his arm, then lowered it to his side.

Instead, he remained beside her and slightly behind, like a shadow. Having the large man in such close proximity should have unnerved her. Previous experience gave her reason to be wary. But Tucker's unnecessary protective presence allowed her to relax her guard a tiny bit.

Lowery's Dress Shop sat kitty corner from the cavalry office, as the crow flies. Tucker wordlessly guided her north on Buckboard Alley rather than by the saloons on Old Cheyenne Road where the volume had increased since the sun set.

Estelle allowed the major to follow her up the stairs that led to the residence on the second floor. Nerves quivered in her stomach. She'd never met Aunt Millie, who wasn't a true blood relative, but the woman sent gifts from time to time. Sweet dresses she barely wore and a soft doll with woolen yarn hair were among Estelle's treasured memories of her mysterious aunt.

She had one dress packed in the bottom of her satchel at the livery. She wished she'd taken the time to change. Too late now. She raised her hand and knocked on the door.

"I'm comin', I'm comin'. There's not a sewing emergency in the world that can't wait till tomorrow." Came a muffled voice from inside. Then clearer she heard, "Who is it?" as if the woman's face was pressed against the crack in the door.

"I'm Estelle. I'm lookin' for Millie Lowery. I mean Mildred Lowery. You knew my mother."

Metal scraped against wood as the door was unlatched. It opened enough for the woman's head to come through. She peered at Estelle and spoke in a whisper. "Amber?" She blinked twice, then opened the door all the way, allowing the lamplight from inside to spill onto the landing. "Estelle, is it truly you, child?"

Estelle bit her lip and nodded as tears threatened to fall. "It's me, Aunt Millie. I need your help."

"Aren't you the vision of your mother? Come here." Mildred opened her arms and Estelle went to her, crouching awkwardly to embrace the much shorter woman.

Estelle choked out a single sob before drawing in a deep breath and stepping back. A hanky appeared at her elbow, reminding her of her unwelcome escort. She accepted the cloth and dabbed the unshed tears from her eyes.

"And who're you?" Mildred snapped at Major Tucker. She turned back to Estelle. "What kind of trouble are you in?"

"It's not me. It's Wabli. This is Major Tucker. He's helping us."

"A pleasure to make your acquaintance, ma'am." Tucker tipped his hat and half-bowed.

"Hmm. Pretty eastern manners won't work on me.

41

Both you, get in here. No use givin' the neighbors a show."

Mildred settled them both at the dining table and put out a half loaf of bread and crock of butter. "I wish I had more, but I only cook for one now and don't often have leftovers."

"This is more than enough, Auntie," Estelle reassured her, and Tucker added his agreement and thanks.

She placed the kettle on to heat and joined her guests. "I was sorry to hear about your ma. Thank you for writing me. I'll miss her letters and readin' about her exciting life."

Estelle snorted. "I'm sure Mamma embellished. There was a great deal more drudgery than excitement."

Mildred clicked her tongue. "For an old woman like me it was plenty. I enjoyed watching you young'uns grow through her descriptions, too." The kettle whistled and she rose to serve tea. "Now, enough maudlin topics. Tell me why you're here. You runnin' from—"

Estelle interrupted. She didn't want the major involved in their family problems as well. "It's Wabli. He came here and got arrested for horse thievin'."

"Not, technically, arrested," Major Tucker interjected. "Detained. Captain Dooley doesn't have the authority to arrest anyone, especially a civilian."

Mildred turned a glare on him. "Then just let him out." The word *fool* wasn't added to the order but certainly implied.

Estelle placed her hand on the older woman's arm. "It's turned more complicated than that. The sheriff recommended we sit tight until the circuit judge arrives."

Mildred pursed her lips. "Mmpft. Hanson."

The major picked up the explanation. "The sheriff's right. I don't like it but freeing your nephew will cause more problems than it would solve, for everyone. My goal is to get Wabli out of this without a court record."

"What are you, some kind of lawyer?" Mildred glared at him again.

"Yes, Auntie. Like I said, he's helping."

"Mmpft. Fancy eastern lawyer, likely." She turned back to Estelle. "What can I do to help?"

"I need a place to stay. I understand if you don't have room. I wanted to come see you anyway. I'd been plannin' on it since before all this happened."

Mildred glanced around her home. "I used to have more space. After Horace passed, I had the spare bedroom and part of the parlor turned into apartments to let. There are stairs on the other side of the building."

"Mamma said she stayed in an apartment behind the dress shop."

"So she did. My washer woman stays there now. Your mamma was the first one to have that job. I'd watch you sometimes when you got fussy while she tried to work. I didn't mind. You had my Race wrapped around your dainty little finger, too." She smiled tenderly at the memory.

"He died a few years later, didn't he? Mamma spoke of him fondly."

"Yes. Yes, he did, the rascal." She blinked away tears. "I appreciate your mamma naming Wabli after him. Meant a lot to me."

"I remember the fit his father threw. He'd never heard of a Lakota with the middle name Horace." Estelle laughed, though it had been a bit scary at the time, watching the big Lakota rant at her mother.

"I'm glad she stuck to her guns. I know—"

"She was glad to honor Uncle Race that way and Wabli wears the name proudly."

Mildred glanced at the major who, no doubt, paid closer attention to the conversation than he appeared. "One of my rent rooms is free right now. My seamstress up and married and moved out, then my niece stayed there. She met a beau and moved out, too. Come to think it, the room might be jinxed." She cut a glare at the major. "But please, stay as my guest."

Estelle shook her head. "Oh no, I couldn't. Let me pay you rent. Or I can sleep on a pallet in here someplace."

Standing, Mildred picked up the empty teacups and plates. "My mind's made up. I'll not hear another word about it. You know better than to argue with your elders." She placed everything on the countertop and walked to the door. She threw a shawl over her shoulders and removed a key on a string from a hook. "Well, come along. I'm to bed soon, and I'll see you settled first."

Estelle rose before Major Tucker could pull out her chair. He retrieved both of their hats from the coatrack and handed her hers. They'd not bothered to remove their jackets.

"Come up for breakfast at six. I'll have more questions then." Mildred ushered them out the door.

"Yes, Aunt Millie. We'll talk more then."

Mildred turned a knowing eye on her niece. "We certainly will. We can discuss your ridiculous attire then, too." She trod deftly down the stairs leaving her guests to follow in her wake.

Chapter 7

After retrieving Estelle's bags from the livery at Mrs. Lowery's behest, Tucker stopped by Jake's Place on the way back to the cavalry office. He accepted the dry, crusty remains of whatever the night's special had been and renegotiated his and Wabli's meal delivery. He wouldn't cut Cecil out of a job, and he appreciated the sheriff paying for Wabli's meals, but from now on, he'd pay for the boy's and his own. If he happened to be out of the office at mealtime, he didn't think it would be a hardship for Wabli to eat double.

He'd been gone well over an hour. This would be a true test of Wabli's character. Tucker hoped his instincts wouldn't prove wrong and the boy would be ensconced in his room as instructed.

As he approached, two soldiers stumbled across his path. One noticed the presence of a superior officer and attempted a salute, only to lose his balance and fall into his friend. Tucker grabbed the oblivious private's collar and jerked him upright. The man came up with a lazy swing of his fist, which Tucker sidestepped.

Tucker gave him a shake. "Do you really want a court martial on your record before you reach your first posting?" If this typified the behavior allowed under Captain Dooley, no wonder the townsfolk and sheriff were upset. He released the drunkard and turned to the other who still practiced at a proper salute. "Take your friend to the barracks. Both of you report to me first thing in the morning. What are your names?"

"I'm Smith, sir, and he's Conners." Smith looped his arm around his friend's waist.

"Get out of here, private. Eight o'clock tomorrow morning. Don't be late and don't be hung over." He continued to the main office, next door to the barracks. A lamp still burned on the desk, but he didn't detect any other movement through the window. Wabli had either followed his instruction or flown the coop. He let himself in and crossed the room. The dinner basket sat on the desk next to the lamp and Wabli's door was closed.

He knocked lightly on the door. "I'm back. Do you need anything else tonight?"

The door opened a crack and the boy peered out. "I don't need anything. I'm not a guest."

Tucker removed his hat. "You're not exactly a prisoner either. I'll be across the hall." The office wasn't the place for a prisoner of detained guest, yet Dooley saw fit to lock the kid up in there. Fool.

Wabli gave him a solemn look before shutting the door. The boy appeared wise beyond his years. It would help him through this situation and make it easier for Tucker to aid his exoneration.

With a frustrated sigh. He turned to the room he would use for the next few days. He hung his hat on a peg and draped his jacket on the back of a chair. He found clean sheets in a cabinet and prepared his bed by rote while he went over the day's problems in his head. Egad, it had been a long day! His two-to-three-day detour in Wylder looked like it could stretch out to a week. It all depended on how fast the circuit judge traveled. Tucker hated when any aspect of an assignment was beyond his control.

Between the judge, Wabli, Dooley, and Estelle, he didn't know where to start wrangling things back in order. Dooley was easiest to deal with. Tucker had regulations and protocol to support his decisions. He could only help Estelle as much as she'd allow. It bothered him most that he wanted to involve himself in her problems at all.

He wasn't attracted to her. Not really. Of course, she was beautiful and full of life, but he preferred gently bred females like his sister's friends. His mother's last letter indicated there were several anxiously awaiting his return.

He mostly felt pity for Estelle and her brother. They were about to head off into the world with no practical knowledge of how it worked. The boy's first time away from the Wild West Show and he managed to get himself arrested, for goodness sake. The two would not have an easy time of it.

Estelle held nothing more than a passing curiosity. Any man would have noticed her. He slipped under the bed covers, allowing sleep to claim him before his brain forced him to prob his feeling any deeper.

****

Tucker glared at the dusty rolls of paper stashed haphazardly in the cubbies. Performing the audit amounted to busy work. Work that Captain Dooley should have been busy doing daily, but obviously hadn't for several months, or perhaps years.

Wabli emerged from his room, Tucker refused to consider it a cell, and leaned against the door frame. At his side, a hand held a checkered napkin. The other hand turned a fried chicken leg as his teeth gnawed every edible bit. "Are you going to clean it?" He asked, nodding to the shelf.

"No. I have to sort it, audit it, and bind it into submission." Tucker sighed. He didn't even know where to start.

Wabli smirked. "How does the audit work?"

"These are records of all the men and supplies that come through this office. I need to match all the invoices with their outgoing counterparts. Sometimes a supply order will have to be split three or four ways to be picked up by the forts we service. I have to make sure the split numbers add up to the original whole." Tucker selected a roll of papers off the bottom shelf and carried it to the window. He opened it, held the roll outside, and blew, sending dust into the chilly November air. He set the roll on the desk and pulled a hanky out of his pocket to blow his nose. He could not think of a worse way to spend his last weeks in the U.S. Cavalry…well, there *were* worse ways.

Stripping away the last morsel of meat, Wabli tossed the leg bone in the trash can. It landed with a *tink* in the metal can. He wiped his hands and face with the napkin and placed it back in Cecil's basket. "Want some help? I can read and I'm good with numbers."

Tucker glanced at his charge and forced himself to look with new eyes. Instead of a grubby half-Indian boy, he tried to see a young man as full of potential as he'd once been. Surprisingly, it wasn't difficult. "I could probably use a second set of eyes. Thank you."

Smith and Conners neglected to show up at the assigned time that morning. The threat of court martial was an empty one, but they didn't know that. He eyed the dusty rolls of paper again. When they finally dragged their hungover carcasses in, Tucker had the perfect job ready for them.

Chapter 8

A hand rested on Estelle's back on top of the bedcovers. She kept her eyes closed and struggled to control her breathing. Moist breath on the back of her neck moved to her ear and the thin mattress of her camp bed dipped as a knee came down beside her hip. He spoke curt, guttural words, but she couldn't make them out. She could never make them out.

The hand moved from her back and slid to her breast, squeezing it through her night dress. She bit her lip to keep from screaming. If he thought she slept, he might leave. Though no one would be able to sleep through such rough handling.

She opened her eyes, hoping to see hints of dawn creeping through the flaps of the tent. Daylight meant people and activity. It was still too dark to see the brown canvas wall in front of her face. The hand slipped under the blanket and glided down her stomach and hip. The fingers pinched the hem of her nightgown and began to tow it up her leg.

Estelle jolted upright. It wasn't dark and no one invaded her bed. If only the terrifying memory would cease to invade her nightmares, she'd rest easier.

She'd overslept. Hopefully Auntie would forgive her this one time. She needed to get moving, though. Wabli waited and she wanted to talk to Aunt Millie about her mother's journal. They may not be able to stay in town long after Wabli's release. She planned to use the interim time to solve the mystery of her parentage. Her existence began in Wylder; the answers were here to be uncovered.

She'd learned to quickly throw off the remnants of the nightmare. Dwelling on the memory and fearing over the future served no purpose. Best to move forward. Yanking on clean trousers from her bag, she donned a green floral calico blouse to top it. Her mother always told her it brought out the gold in her eyes. She hoped her aunt would be so pleased with the shirt's ruffled accents, she'd not fuss about Estelle's choice of legwear.

After splashing cold water on her face, braiding her hair, slipping on her buckskin coat, and pocketing Flora, she hurried downstairs to greet her aunt.

Two ladies bustled out of the dress shop as Estelle approached. They spared her disdainful looks as they exited the porch and turned toward the mercantile. She wasn't here to please the townsfolk. She shrugged, turning the knob, and entered the store.

Mildred looked up from her work. "If you want hot breakfast, you need to be up by six. I left oats in the pot upstairs. They'll be cold now. There's fresh bread. Could have had it warm too, had you not lazed in bed all morning. Travel wears a person out. I'll give you today, but don't make it a habit."

Estelle gave the woman a tentative kiss on her dry cheek. "Yes, auntie. It won't happen again. Thank you." She headed to the interior stairs that led to Mildred's apartment.

"See that it doesn't. When you're done, come back down here and we'll visit."

****

"Well, darn. I'm outta tea leaves." Mildred replaced the tin's lid and plunked it down on her worktable. "I don't even remember using the last of 'em," she grumbled under her breath. She looked at Estelle. "Might as well introduce you around. We'll take a quick trip to the mercantile. Can't have our chat without tea."

Estelle waited while her aunt retrieved her cloak and turned the sign in the front window. With the empty tin held tight in her hand, Mildred led Estelle around the corner to the Wylder Mercantile. The bell over the door tinkled happily as the two women entered.

Mildred set the tin on the wooden countertop. "One scoop of oolong, please, Finn."

"Just opening a new shipment, Mrs. Lowery. I have a crate of yard goods with your name on it as well."

She tapped the counter with her palm. "Very good, Finn. I've been waiting for that. I'll nose around a bit while I wait. Be sharp, though. I've got my shop closed up."

The young man smiled. "Yes, ma'am." He slipped into the back room.

"Such a production for tea." She turned to Estelle. "Well, this is the mercantile. Finn Wylder does a fair job of not running it into the ground."

Estelle looked around the store. Glass jars filled with everything from tea to candy to pipe tobacco lined the shelves. In the center of the room, barrels offering apples, potatoes, and other perishables were available to customers to help themselves. A large scale sat on the counter next to a notepad and pencil. When the Wild West Show toured in Ohio Estelle saw big metal tills used in a few stores. New innovations must be slow arriving in Wylder.

She followed her aunt to the far end of the store where household goods were shelved. The mercantile had a few bolts of calico and muslin, but nothing compared to the selection at Lowery's. Her aunt inspected a prominently displayed carpet sweeper.

"Are you going to get one, Auntie?" Estelle had seen the wonder at a fair once. "It says new and improved."

She straightened and turned her back to the sweeper. "Why would I waste my money when a broom works just fine?" She glanced back at the appliance wistfully.

The shop bell tinkled again as a stately woman entered.

"Oh, dear," Mildred muttered.

"Do you know her?" Estelle whispered.

"She's a friend of sorts. Look sharp." Her aunt stepped in front of her and walked toward the newcomer. "Una! How good to see you. It saves me a trip to bring my niece around for introductions."

Una's head snapped around at Mildred's greeting. Her gaze shot to Estelle and her lips curved in a sly smile. "Why, Millie, you silly goose. I already know Sarah."

"Not Sarah. This is Estelle; she's Gilda's daughter." Mildred smiled tightly.

Una's eyes lit up. "Oh! Gilda, the girl who used to work as a—"

"As my washer woman, years ago. Yes. She passed recently." She slid aside so Estelle could stand next to her. "Estelle, this is Una Barlow."

She eyed Estelle, taking in her trousers and coat. "You poor, poor dear. Wearing sack cloth hasn't been a mourning tradition since biblical times. I'm sure a visit with Millie will cheer you right up."

Estelle smiled, ignoring the rude remark. "I'm sure

I'll enjoy getting reacquainted with Aunt Millie." No need to mention that the last time they were acquainted, Estelle wore nappies. Her aunt seemed to guard herself and weigh her words with this woman. She'd take her cue from the older woman and not offer any extra information.

Una turned her attention back to Mildred. "I just came from the church. You would not believe what they're trying to get by with at the school."

Estelle had no interest in town gossip, so let her mind wander while the ladies conversed. As anxious as she was to get to the cavalry office and see Wabli, she knew better than to rush her aunt. If Aunt Millie wanted to chat, they would chat. If she needed tea to chat, they would have tea. Trying to rush would be disrespectful, as would acting impatient with Una's gossip.

She trusted Wabli's safety to Major Tucker, even though she ought to consider him the enemy. He'd been bossy, but also kind and fair. Her instincts had protected her in the past. Hopefully they wouldn't fail her now.

"Ambrose is probably rolling in grave if he's watching what's going on. God rest his soul." Una crossed herself.

Estelle became instantly alert. "Who's Ambrose?"

Both women looked at her. Una spoke. "Ambrose is my late husband. He helped build this town. He would be appalled at what's happening. Do you have feelings on the subject? I'm trying to form an opposition group. I could use all the support I can gather."

Her cheeks burned. "Ah, um. I'm not going to be in town long enough to join any causes, but I wish you the very best of luck. Aunt Millie, I'm going to check on your order." She stepped around Una's ample frame and hurried to the counter feeling confused and speculative eyes drilling into her back the whole way.

Chapter 9

Aunt Millie set the saucer and cup down on the small table. The woman knew just how much force to use to cause the tea to slosh angrily but not spill over the rim. She'd obviously hosted many passive aggressive tea parties in the past.

"How about you start by explaining why you lit out of the mercantile like you'd seen a ghost. It was rude and unladylike. You have a lot to overcome in that area as it is." Mildred sat and flicked a napkin open on her lap.

"She was rude first. I don't understand why you're friends with her." Estelle opened her own napkin but hadn't calmed enough to enjoy her tea.

Her aunt glared at her. "I may love you like my own, but you may not come to town and judge my friendships. That said, Una and I have a unique relationship. The last thing you want to do is draw her attention. She'll scent blood on the water, quick as anything."

"That's a strange way to talk about your friends."

"She was one of the first friends I made when I moved to Wylder. She helped me through a tough time. We grew apart. Now we're both widows but at the same time, in very different places in our lives. The woman I am now is not so fond of the woman she's become, but it's in my best interest to stay on her good side. Enough on that topic. You didn't answer my question."

Estelle sighed and pulled her coat from the

chairback. She slid her mother's journal from the pocket. "Even before Wabli came here, I always planned to come see you. This is Mamma's journal. I found it a month ago, not long after she passed. She talks about my father."

Mildred's gaze softened and she accepted the book from her niece. "You know what your mother—"

"I know Mamma worked as a harlot before she moved in with you and Uncle Horace. I knew before I read the journal. She tried real hard to make sure I never had to take that path. But she talks about one special man who—"

"It's not possible for her to have known for certain." She tapped the cover to the journal.

"But she did. She swears it. Or at least she seems dead certain." She held her aunt's gaze. "Just read it. See if you recognize the man."

Her aunt blinked. "I thought you said she knows who it is."

"She never names him. She calls him *A*. I assume it's the first letter of his name or maybe his surname. That's what surprised me at the mercantile. Your friend called her husband *Ambrose*. He would have been alive then."

With a frown, she leaned back in her chair, pensive. "You're suggestin' Ambrose visited your mother at the Social Club while he was married to Una. She caught pregnant around that same time. Ezra's a month or so younger than you."

"I have a brother?" Estelle had never considered the possibility, nor that her father may have been married to someone else. She'd always assumed he worked as a ranch hand or something else that didn't pay well. When her mother wrote of him "not being at a place in his life where he could marry" and her wanting to "preserve his reputation" it never occurred to her the man might be a prominent citizen and adulterer.

"I'm not saying that," she snapped. "Ambrose was quite a few years older than Una. It was a miracle he managed to conceive one child, let alone two around the same time. There were other men around with *A* names."

"Who?" She inched to the edge of her chair. *Please, somebody kind. Not someone who'd cheat on their family.*

Mildred lifted her cup and sipped. She set it down and dabbed her mouth with the napkin. Finally, her shoulders slumped, and she met Estelle's gaze. "I don't know. I can't think of a single person."

****

A billowing cloud of dust greeted Estelle as she approached the cavalry office. In the middle of it, two disheveled soldiers with feather dusters brushed the dust from rolls of papers stacked on a wooden table.

"Can you hold up a minute?" She called to them.

They both paused their work and looked up.

One leered. "Well, hello, pretty la—oof!"

The second soldier elbowed the first in the gut. "That kind of behavior got us stuck out here to begin with," he hissed to his partner. He yanked his hat from his head. "Sorry about that, ma'am. What can I do for you?"

"I'd like to get into the office, please. I have business with Major Tucker."

By then, the dust had somewhat settled. The more polite soldier stepped aside, allowing her to pass. "As you please, ma'am. Have a nice day."

As Estelle climbed the wooden stair and reached for the door, she overheard the first man's snide comments.

"I'll bet she has business with the Major—oof! Cease your abuse!"

"You cease! Just because you can see her legs don't mean she a woman of ill repute. Maybe she ain't got nothin' else to wear. If she reports your behavior to the major, we'll be in even more trouble."

Estelle's cheeks warmed. Her aunt refused to let her leave until she'd measured her for a skirt. She'd never been embarrassed about her attire before. As a celebrity, *Horton's Shooting Star*, in her circle, no one questioned her choice of clothing. Did everyone just assume she wore her costume all the time? She turned the knob and let herself into the office before she overheard anymore humiliating truths.

It relieved her to find Wabli standing behind a table piled high with more paper rolls. Major Tucker's desk sat beneath a similar pile. He pulled more dusty rolls from pigeonhole cubbies and placed them gently in a crate on the floor. Even so, dust particles sifted into the air as the paper settled into place.

The major turned his head to cough, nearly choking when he noticed Estelle standing in the doorway. He rose from his seat, still hacking, and beckoned her in.

"Hey, Stella. You're late this morning," Wabli greeted her.

She resisted the urge to beat the major on his back. Finally, his coughing subsided, and he came around the desk. He pulled a chair over so she could sit across from her brother.

"Sorry about that. We're doing a bit of housekeeping this morning." Every bit the respectable officer this morning, Estelle decided he must have gotten a good night's sleep. The bossy, grumpy man from the night before was absent.

She raised an eyebrow as she sat in the proffered chair. "Free labor?"

"It's that or sit around being bored. I'm not asking him to do anything I'm not doing myself. The punishment is for the men out front dusting."

"What did they do?"

"Let's just say I'm starting to deal with the things Sheriff Hansen mentioned."

"I asked to help," Wabli added. "I already read all the books on the shelves. Even the boring ones. This is figures, it's more fun."

"What are you doing?" Estelle leaned over to look at the piles of paper Wabli had weighted down with rocks so they wouldn't curl.

"Right now, I'm putting everything in order by date. There's paperwork older than three years here!" Wabli's excitement made Estelle smile. He'd always been more interested in academics as opposed to the rough and tumble activities of the other cast members. Mamma argued with Wabli's father about it a lot. Her brother longed to attend regular school and dreamed of one day furthering his education. Ohanzee Cetan Wakuwa wanted him to embrace his Lakota heritage and disavow white man's ways. Wabli wanted to walk in both worlds.

"From about the time Captain Dooley took over the office. I don't think he's bound anything since he started." Tucker gave the mess a frustrated look.

"What happens next?" Estelle asked.

"We match invoices to receipts and then bind it all together in a book for each month." He pointed to a shelf full of books all the same size and color. "Those are some older volumes."

Estelle surveyed the untidy workspace then looked back at the major. "Seems a little below your pay grade."

He gave her an irritated look. "It is. But I'm stuck here until the circuit judge comes through. Besides, my superior officer asked me to perform and audit during my visit. Neither of us realized it would take longer to prepare for the audit as it will to perform it."

The front door opened and Sheriff Hanson ambled in. He removed his hat and nodded at Estelle. "Ma'am." Then he addressed the room. "It's good you're all here; save me a trip. Glad to see you're keepin' the boys too busy to make trouble, Major."

Estelle stood. "He's never been any trouble." *How dare he treat Wabli like a criminal!*

The sheriff gave her a gentle smile. "I was referrin' to the dust beaters out front." He jerked his back toward the door. "But bein' busy never hurt no one and idle hands can get the best of us in trouble at times. Ain't that right, Major Tucker?"

The major met the sheriff's gaze and nodded. "I'd certainly rather be busy than not. What brings you by, Sheriff?"

"Making my rounds, which include stoppin' in at the post and telegraph offices. It appears the judge is delayed. Laid up with the gout. I'd say he's sorry about the imposition, but honestly, he probably don't really care that much." The sheriff hooked his thumbs on his gun belt. "But I'm sorry for it, if it's any consolation."

Wabli's shoulders slumped and the major sighed.

"How long do you think it'll be? Wabli and I can't stay too long." Her gaze involuntarily shot to the front window.

"Hard to say. Maybe a week to treat and another day or two to sober him up. He's in Omaha. If he don't have any other stops, he can be here in three or four days. What's your hurry?" The sheriff pinned her with a hard look, like he could see all her secrets.

Estelle swallowed. The major also watched her. "It's just, well, Wabli will be eighteen in a few months, a legal adult. He's essentially an adult now. I know lots of seventeen-year-olds who own property and are married and such."

"What's your point, ma'am?" The sheriff's gaze never wavered.

"Someone from the Horton's Wild West Show might come lookin' for him. We both worked there with our, with our mother, but we never signed contracts on our own. We didn't take anything with us we didn't own outright from our mother. I don't want Wabli taken advantage of while he's stuck here."

"Stella," Wabli hissed at her. "I can take care of myself."

She turned to him. "You think you can, but the only reason you're here is the color of your skin. You may be able to control your own actions and care for yourself, but you can't control everyone else."

As she turned back to the sheriff, she allowed her eyes to briefly meet Major Tucker's before sliding away. She saw, what she hoped to be kindness, in Sheriff Hanson's impassive expression. "Promise me you won't release Wabli to anyone from Horton's. Promise me you won't let the judge do it either. Please."

A hand touched her arm. Tucker had moved in behind her. "If all your paperwork is in order as you say, they'll have no grounds to take him. I'll be happy to look over any documents they may provide that make claims on either of you. But you can't lie to me. If I find I can't trust you in one thing, I'll assume you can't be trusted in other areas as well."

Estelle looked at the hand touching her arm. It didn't alarm her like that kind of thing normally did the morning after a nightmare. She didn't feel compelled to reach for Flora.

He moved his hand away and stood formally, clasping both hands behind his back.

Weighing her words so she spoke absolute truth, she said, "Horton's Wild West Show has no legal hold on either of us."

"Well, that's good enough for me. Glad you got a fancy attorney to deal with it. My hands are full enough with town business." He replaced his hat and offered a hand to the major. "Much obliged, Major." Tucker grasped the man's hand and responded with a nod. Sheriff Hanson then offered his hand to Wabli. "Son."

Wabli scrambled forward and took the sheriff's hand. "Thank you, sir."

Finally, he turned to Estelle and tipped his hat. "Ma'am."

The door shut behind Sheriff Hanson and Estelle turned to meet her brother's worried glare. She plastered a false smile on her lips. "See, everything will be just fine."

Chapter 10

Tucker sensed strife between the siblings, and after a tense, whispered conversation, Estelle took her leave with a promise to be back later. He and Wabli worked companionably all afternoon until Cecil delivered an early dinner from Jake's.

Tucker wiped the last bit of food residue from his plate with his hunk of bread. Studying Wabli as he finished his meal, Tucker took two bowls of cobbler out of the basket and replaced them with the dirty plates to be collected later.

"What are your plans after we get you released?" Tucker asked.

Wabli scooped a huge spoonful of dessert in his mouth and shrugged. They'd talked earlier about proper responses to questions, but Tucker allowed the boy to formulate a better answer while he chewed. He swallowed audibly and drank down half his glass of buttermilk before answering.

"I'll go wherever Estelle wants, I suppose." He shrugged again.

"I'm interested in what you want to do. You're old enough to be on your own in many parts of this country. I was studying law at your age." Tucker took a bite of his own cobbler. Jake certainly had a way with sweets. The flaky crust melted in his mouth and the apples were just the right amount of tart and sweet.

Wabli's eyes lit up for a moment. Tucker almost missed it. The boy had a dream tucked away in his heart. "I don't know. Help my people, I guess. I don't want to perform; I know that."

"Help your people how? You realize, even though you look Indian through and through, you're fifty percent white. Estelle's your people, I'm your people, too." Tucker reminded him. The boy would have obstacles in the way of reaching his goals. He didn't need to lend credence to the ones inside his head.

Wabli shook his head. "Don't matter. Estelle's right. As long as I look like this, no one will listen."

"Tell me what you want for your people?"

"I want the Lakotas to be able to have a safe place to live and practice their traditions. Part of the reason so many Lakotas joined *Horton's* was so they could stay in touch with their heritage. But half of what they do is pretend to attack settlers' cabins and rampage. I hate it!" His voice was laced with grief and frustration.

Tucker had seen other wild west shows when they'd performed near places he'd been stationed. The skits Wabli referred to had unsettled him. He'd experienced similar scenarios in real life and didn't understand why anyone would want to recreate such a thing for entertainment.

Wabli continued. "But I like to watch when the Lakotas do traditional dancing. And when they sit around the fire at night, I like to listen to their stories, most of them anyway. I don't like the stories about tribes being cheated out of their land and forced to move farther and farther west."

"What did you do in the show?" Tucker finished his cobbler and put the bowl in the basket.

"Pony races, mostly. I did a lot of behind-the-scenes jobs, too, and cared for the horses."

"What made you come to Wylder?" Tucker asked, though he couldn't think of any better options for the youth. The boy was right. He would always be judged first by the way he looked. This whole situation was a case in point.

"I knew Estelle planned to come." He studied his bowl intently, not meeting Tucker's gaze.

"She was frantic looking for you when she arrived. Why did you leave without her? Why didn't you tell her you were leaving in the first place?" *What aren't you telling me, Wabli?*

"They planned to train me to be in the skits. I would make more money and I could keep doing my other tasks as well. But I didn't want to pretend to hurt people or burn cabins or take scalps."

Tucker prodded more. "Why did Estelle want to leave?"

"You'll have to ask her that." Wabli pursed his lips; a physical representation of figuratively buttoning up. There were a lot of holes in the story, holes he wanted filled.

Time to move on. He'd glean no new information that afternoon. With Wabli's eager and competent help, they'd sorted all the loose papers into piles by month. "Are you ready to get back to work, or would you rather quit for the day and start again in the morning?"

Wabli glanced out the window. "It's not even dark yet and Stella said she'd be back. Might as well keep going."

"Why don't you work on 1878 and I'll go back to the beginning of this mess, 1875? You're comparing the incoming shipments to the receipts showing how much of the supplies went to each fort. Even if some stayed here, there should be a receipt for it."

Sometime later, Estelle strode into the office, bringing with her a gust of cold air. Tucker looked up from his work, surprised that dusk had settled.

"It's late, Stell. I thought you'd gone home." Wabli frowned.

Estelle removed her hat and smoothed down the tendrils of hair that failed to conform. "I promised I'd be back. I was helping Aunt Millie and Leona and lost track of time. I wanted to come and check on you before heading back for dinner."

"I'm fine. I'm helping with important work. You didn't need to come check on me like a child."

Hurt flashed across her face. Tucker wanted to reprimand Wabli for being so harsh with his sister, but it wasn't his place. Whatever they had argued about earlier apparently still brewed between them.

"If you're too busy to visit, I'll come by in the morning. Goodnight, brother," she said, but made no motion to leave.

Wabli sighed and put down the papers he held. He walked to his sister and put his arms around her. "I'm sorry. I appreciate you looking out for me, but I'm really doing fine here. The major won't let me get in too much trouble."

Estelle squeezed him in return. "I'm sorry, too, Little Eagle. I'll try not to mother you as much." She eased out of his embrace. "I'll see you tomorrow."

Tucker set his papers down. "I'll walk you."

"There's really no need. I'm not going very far." Estelle replaced her hat.

"It's dark, Stell. Let him walk with you."

She glanced up at Tucker. "Fine. Let's go."

They encountered several soldiers as they stepped onto the street. The men immediately straightened and saluted Tucker.

"Gentlemen, where are you headed this evening?" He asked.

"The saloon, sir," one corporal replied.

"Be on your best behavior, men. Smith and Conners can tell you about what happens if you're not." Tucker made a point to look each man in the eye.

"We will, sir. They did, sir."

Tucker nodded. "What's Captain Dooley doing this evening?"

"He appeared to be writing a letter, sir."

"Thank you, gentlemen. Enjoy yourselves." He turned to Estelle and offered her his arm. To his surprise, she wrapped tentative fingers around his forearm. He felt the warmth on his skin, though she kept her touch light.

"I appreciate you makin' Wabli feel useful," she said.

"He's doing real work and will help me have the audit done in half the time. I know the circumstances are unfortunate for you both, but I'm grateful for a second set trustworthy of eyes. He also makes a better roommate than Captain Dooley." Tucker grinned, hoping to make her feel more at ease, though he didn't understand why it was important to him.

"Well, I thank you, at any rate." Estelle didn't look at him, but her hand relaxed into his arm, sending tendrils of warmth up to his shoulder.

"What are your plans tomorrow?" he blurted.

She paused and looked up at his outburst, a puzzled

expression on her face. "I have an errand to run in the morning, then I need to take Starlight out for some real exercise."

"That's a good idea. Maybe I'll join you with Demon." Providing the horse was willing to cooperate.

Estelle stopped and pulled her hand from his sleeve. He missed her touch at once. "I don't recall inviting you to join us."

"It's not safe to ride alone." He reached for her hand, but she evaded.

She put her hands on her hips. "I have almost always ridden alone anywhere I wanted to go. I've been doing it for nearly ten years."

"In cities and places you're recognized as a celebrity. Not here, where folks only see a woman wearing trousers riding alone. Where do you intend to ride?" He tamped down his frustration at her naivety.

"East of town; out past the livery. I noticed the area from the train. It looked deserted and perfectly safe." Her nose tipped up slightly, daring him to disagree.

"Deserted, as in no one would hear you scream. Anyone could follow you."

"Argh!" She placed both hands on Tucker's chest and shoved.

He was ready for her this time. He grasped both of her wrists and pulled her with him when he took a step back. She fell against his chest, breathing heavily and curling her fingers into fists. When she tried to beat them against him, he held her steady.

He bent so his lips were close to her ear. She stilled and her breath caught. He lowered his tone and spoke. "You won't let Wabli go off on his own because he looks full Indian and you don't want him hurt or in a worse situation than he's in now. Doesn't it occur to you that people will treat you poorly or take advantage of you simply because you're female? There are evil people who will harass a man by himself. Why wouldn't those people do the same and worse to a lone woman?"

He continued to hold her wrists as he slowly eased back, making sure she had her balance before releasing her. "I've never met a woman so fiercely independent to the point of stupidity."

She scowled at him, rubbing her wrists, though Tucker knew he hadn't gripped too tightly. She spun on her boot heel and stomped toward the dress shop.

Tucker followed a few feet behind and watched till she was upstairs and behind her locked door. Why did he insist on riling her? Why did she insist on behaving in a way that made it necessary? Either way, he knew where he'd be come mid-morning.

He schooled his expression before going back into the office. He didn't understand what was going on between himself and Estelle. Until he did, Wabli certainly didn't need to worry about it.

The boy looked up at his arrival. "There's something not right."

Chapter 11

When Estelle arrived on time for breakfast the next morning, her aunt greeted her with an unexpected gift.

"Um, thank you, Auntie. What is it?" She held the garment out in front of her.

"It's a compromise. I know I can't force you into a dress and I don't have time to go over all the ins and outs of behavin' like a lady when you wear one. This is a split skirt. When you're standin' still, it will give the appearance of a regular skirt but will still allow you to ride easily. You mentioned exercising your horse today." She brushed a bit of lint off the lightweight wool.

Estelle didn't have the energy or the heart to argue with the woman to whom she owed much. She laid it carefully over the chair back and sat down at the table. "Thank you. I'll change after we break our fast."

Mildred nodded. "You're welcome." She proceeded to scoop oats into both of their bowls.

Stifling a yawn, Estelle dug in. Her aunt wasn't much for idle chitchat, which suited her mood just fine. She awoke naturally instead of with the nightmare of the previous morning. Unfortunately, it had taken her a long time the night before to settle her restless mind.

She fumed at the major's words, more so at the truth to them. The world outside of Horton's Wild West show could be a dangerous place. Dangers existed inside as well, she thought ruefully.

The other thing that kept her from sleep was her reaction to Major Tucker's manhandling. To be fair, she started it in her fit of temper. Why did he rile her so? The whole encounter had her confused and uncomfortable.

His hold had been rough in response to her attempted shove, but gentle at the same time. He restricted her movement and spoke so close to her ear she could feel his breath. But he didn't cause her to panic, didn't induce nightmares.

Quite the opposite, in fact. Major James Tucker's voice, the caress of his fingers on her skin, and his woodsy clean smell peppered her dreams.

"Are you feeling well? You look flushed. Maybe you shouldn't go out today; the temperature's dropped a bit." Mildred put a cool hand on Estelle's cheek.

More heat rushed to her face and neck. "I'm fine, Auntie. Just excited to see Starlight, promise."

"Humph. Well, don't overdo it. I don't have time to tend the sick."

"Yes, ma'am."

"I've given some thought to your search for your father. As much as I loath to suggest it, you may need to talk to Adelaide Willowby at the Social Club." Mildred collected the empty bowls and moved to the dishpan.

"Mamma spoke of her fondly. While she gave me your name as my middle name, our surname, Adleton, came from her. I don't know if she's aware."

"Likely not. Your mother didn't call herself that until after she left. But when I saw she signed her letters that way, without mention of a husband, I guessed that's where it came from."

"I'll stop there after my ride." Estelle collected her new split skirt from the chair back.

Mildred shook her head. "No, that won't do. It will be too late in the afternoon by then. You'll go tomorrow between ten and noon. It's the safest time, no customers."

Estelle hid her grin behind her hand. She loved her aunt despite her surliness. "As you say. Thank you."

****

It might be too early to call. The English actresses she knew used to go on about proper etiquette and how morning calls didn't actually happen until the afternoon. Stuff and nonsense. Surely Wylder, Wyoming, didn't subscribe to such silly rules. If ten in the morning was an appropriate time to call at the Social Club, it was probably a good time to call on Una Barlow, too. Respectable women would be up and about far earlier than prostitutes, Estelle assumed.

She climbed the white stairs to the white front porch of the white house. Her aunt described it as the most pretentious on Buckboard Alley, and white. So very white, with the exception of the shutters and front door, which were painted glossy black. Estelle took a deep breath and knocked.

She heard a hacking cough and a man called out. "Hold your horses. I'm coming."

Resisting the urge to flee, Estelle clenched her fists at her side. Her aunt said Una Barlow was a widow. Could she be keeping company with a man? The door flew open and a man close to her own age leaned against the doorframe.

As fair-haired as Una, the man bore more than a striking resemblance to the older woman. The features that hadn't aged well on Mrs. Barlow were, surprisingly, not unattractive on this gentleman who was, very possibly, her son. If not for his shoeless, unkempt appearance and slimy leer, he'd be quite a catch.

"Well, good morning, darlin'." His gaze slithered over Estelle's body, and she forced herself not to shudder. "Whatever you're selling, I'm most definitely buying." He had the audacity to add a wink.

She steeled her spine. "I'm here to see Mrs. Barlow."

"I'm so sorry. Mother hasn't made an appearance yet this morning. Why don't you come on inside and I'll see if I can be of assistance?" He stepped aside, beckoning her into the home.

"Wait. Mrs. Barlow is your mother?" Her stomach turned at the lecher's obvious interest in her as a woman.

A wide smile crossed his stubbly face. "You must be new around here." He held out his hand, and Estelle placed hers in it. Instead of shaking it, he turned it and brought her inner wrist to his lips. She yanked her hand back, causing his grin to widen. "Ezra Barlow, at your service. Come on in."

Estelle shifted back. "Ah, no. I'll come back another time." She turned and started down the stairs, then stopped to look back. "Is Ambrose Barlow your father?"

Ezra blinked and his smile fled as he adopted a pious air. "That he was. God rest his soul." He clasped a hand to his chest and his eyes turned heavenward.

She hurried down the final steps and headed in the direction of the livery.

"Wait!" Ezra called. He came out onto the porch, prevented from following by his lack of footwear. "You didn't tell me your name."

Ignoring the man who might be her brother, Estelle quickened her pace.

Chapter 12

After spending the morning with Wabli poring over documents, Tucker went straight to the telegraph office. He wired his friend, Major McClure, at Fort Laramie, as well as the receiving clerks at Fort Collins and Fort Russell. The messages had been costly, but Tucker didn't have time to wait on the mail service.

He'd left Wabli recording all their findings. It's not the way others might handle it, letting a civilian, and technically a detainee, be privy to military secrets. But the boy was bored. He'd been the one to discover the discrepancies in the first place, and Tucker could care less who knew how many *top secret* sacks of oats and flour each fort was supposed to get.

Wabli barely looked up from his task when Tucker told him he was leaving to send the wires, then exercise his horse. He appreciated the boy's work ethic. He chose not to mention his plans also included catching up to Estelle.

Now, fighting to keep Demon in check, he rode toward the livery.

Chet Daniels, the owner, stood outside chatting with a man in a wagon. He glanced over and did a double take at Tucker's snorting beast. "Major, what can I do ya for? I, ah, don't know if I got enough space right now for your animal."

Amused, Tucker reassured Chet. "Don't worry.

He's got a stall at the warehouse. I wouldn't subject you to the likes of this one. I'm looking for Miss Adleton. She planned to ride today." He leaned forward in the saddle to prevent Demon from unseating him.

A look of relief crossed Daniels' face, then he narrowed his eyes. "She didn't mention anyone would be joining her."

Tucker would appreciate the man's protectiveness if he wasn't already trying to protect her from her own questionable decisions. "I know she planned to ride out east of town. I didn't think it was a good idea for a woman alone."

Daniels' gaze flitted from Tucker's corded Hardee hat, to his shoulder boards, and finally to his polished boots. Evidently convinced of Tucker's honorable intentions, he jerked his head eastward. "Left about thirty minutes ago."

Tucker tipped his hat. "Much obliged." And finally gave Demon his head.

Before too long, a lone rider appeared in the distance. Woman and horse, all in shades of tan and cream, appeared golden in the autumn sunlight. Despite his genteel upbringing, Tucker rarely waxed poetic, and his reaction to the sight surprised him. He spurred Demon onward.

Estelle had to have heard his approach, but she didn't turn. Her horse shied when Demon got too near, but still she only calmed the palomino with a pat on the neck. To Tucker's chagrin, the foolhardy woman reached over and greeted Demon with a scratch on the nose.

"Anyone could accost you, take you by surprise, out here on your own," Tucker addressed Estelle's back.

"I love it out here. Look." She waved her arm at the vista. "A person can see for miles and miles, all the way to the mountains. No one is going to sneak up on me."

"I snuck up on you."

She finally turned to look at him. "Do you really think I didn't hear you coming?"

"No." Tucker looked out across the prairie, trying to see the beauty Estelle spoke of. "What do you find beautiful about it?"

"It makes me feel powerful, I guess, in control. 'I am monarch of all I survey.'" She laughed. "Silly, I know."

Tucker blinked, surprised she'd be familiar with the quote. "The more you can see, the more in control you feel, I suppose."

Estelle nodded. "Exactly so." She faced the expanse again. "You sound like you disagree."

"It makes me feel the opposite. It's flat, so I can see a great distance, and in all that distance, I see nothing. No resources, no shelter, and if enemies were to appear, no help and no cover. It's not like that where I come from. The only thing I can compare it to is the sea. It makes me feel the same way. It's why I chose the cavalry instead of the navy." He'd never before put into words his reasons for disliking the west so much.

Estelle turned to him. "It makes you feel powerless," she summarized.

"Exactly so." They both smiled as their gazes met. "Will you tell what you've been keeping from me?"

She gave him her back once again and bumped her legs on her horse's sides, bringing her around so they faced each other.

Demon shifted restlessly underneath him, eager to

run again. "Shall we walk while you tell me?"

She nodded and he turned Demon around, so they rode side by side. They walked parallel to Wylder. He'd run Demon again before returning.

"I'll tell you why I wanted to come to Wylder." She rode as one with her horse. Tucker noticed for the first time she wasn't wearing normal trousers but some sort of wide leg pant that resembled a skirt. It was more feminine than her usual attire and suited her.

"That sounds like the answer to a different question than the one I asked."

"It's the one I'm willing to share right now." She kept her eyes trained ahead.

"Very well. Your brother said he knew you'd planned to come here. Your mother came from Wylder." He figured he'd start her off with what he already knew.

She let out a wry laugh. "My mother *came* from Georgia with a man struck by gold fever. He left her in Wylder with no means to return home or for anything else."

"What did she do?"

"What many women do when they are left completely without options in a world controlled by men. She found a job in a fledgling town that offered only one viable option for a pretty young woman." Her expression was stony.

"The Social Club." Now it made sense that Estelle craved power and control. She learned from her mother what it was like to have neither.

"Yes."

"I don't understand why you'd come here. It can't hold any happy memories."

"My mother was a prostitute. My father was a

78

customer. *I* was born here. Wylder is where *I'm* from. We left when I was a baby, so I have no memories of it. Mamma kept in contact with Aunt Millie, Mildred Lowery. She's not my blood aunt, but she took Mamma in when the club kicked her out in the street."

It finally began to sink in just how different Estelle was from the society girls Tucker knew. A rough, bold, bastard daughter of a prostitute. His mother would have a fit if he brought her home. And why did his mind immediately jump to the idea of bringing her home?

She continued. "So, you see, it's really no use trying to gussy me up and turn me into a lady. I'm a lost cause in that respect and perfectly capable the way I am."

Tucker found it interesting she used the word *capable* instead of happy. She may be the most capable women he'd ever encountered, but he found himself wanting her to be happy, too. To make her happy himself. "You refused to answer my first question and now you've neglected to answer your own substitute question."

This time her laugh was bright instead of cynical. "I got off track, didn't I? In short, I'm here to find my father."

Tucker turned to find her smiling at him. "How in the world do you plan to do that?"

"My mother's diary talks about him, one man in particular. She refers to him as my father, so she must have had a way of knowing. She calls him *A*. I don't know his real name, but I assume *A* is the first letter."

It seemed like a harebrained scheme, but he knew better than to criticize. She'd never open up to him again. "What will you do once you find him?"

Estelle shrugged. "I guess that depends on what kind

of man he is."

****

After another run, they rode back to town. Tucker left Estelle at the livery to care for Starlight while he dealt with his own mount. She caught up with him as he entered the cavalry office.

Wabli was still hard at work. Tucker looked over the papers, pleased with the boy's clear and concise penmanship. The siblings visited, then Tucker escorted Estelle back to the dress shop, though it wasn't yet dark.

"My brother looks up to you. I hope he doesn't come to regret it." Worry lines etched her features.

"He's an incredibly bright and curious young man. I enjoy working with him. He's a credit to the time your mother put into educating him. You both are."

Estelle ducked her head.

"As for regret. Even if the judge doesn't dismiss the case, as he should, I'm prepared to stand as a character witness and more if necessary." It was too soon to tell her the kernel of an idea he'd been entertaining about sponsoring Wabli so he could further his education.

"Thank you for believing in him. Not many people would."

"It's an honor." They stopped in the alley by the stairs to her aunt's apartment. "I enjoyed riding with you today, despite being uninvited."

One side of her lips curved into a smirk. "I did as well, to my surprise. You're nearly pleasant to be around when you're not ordering me about."

Without thinking, he raised his hand and traced his finger down her cheek. "Someone should. Keeping you out of trouble could be a full-time job."

Her lips parted at his caress and a small gasp

escaped in response to his comment. He feared he'd overstepped. She sidled away but a small smile graced her face, causing him to sigh in relief.

"Goodnight, Major."

"Rest well, Miss Adleton."

Chapter 13

For the second time in as many days, Estelle found herself climbing onto the porch of a grand home. Oddly, given its purpose, or perhaps because of it, this one seemed more inviting than the Barlow home. The homey appeal of the aged clapboards was much more restful than the pristine white.

It was quieter than any bawdy house she'd ever seen, and she'd encountered many in her travels with the show. Though this may have been due to the time of day; the reason her aunt told her to come between ten and noon.

Hopefully she'd find answers here instead of more questions and a possible brother. She raised her hand and knocked.

****

"Aoife, bring tea, please," Adelaide Willowby called down the hallway as she escorted Estelle into her office. "Do have a seat. Shall we speak of the mundane while we wait on refreshments?"

Estelle sat in the chair the madam indicated, sinking into the brocade cushion. She wished she'd taken Aunt Millie's advice and worn the split skirt again. Adelaide Willowby was Estelle's opposite. Her perfectly coiffed flaxen hair looked to be spun by angels. She was beautiful enough to *be* an angel if Estelle didn't know what she did for a living.

The woman cleared her throat. Estelle had been wool gathering. Her cheeks burned.

"You've the look of your mother." Adelaide's steady gaze seemed to observe Estelle's every twitch. She tried to sit still, but the chair had her at a disadvantage.

"So I've heard," she mumbled.

"Gracious. That's where the resemblance ends. Sit up and stop mumbling. I know your mother taught you better than that." She turned her head when a woman appeared at the door. "Thank you, Aoife. You remember Amber, don't you? This is her daughter, Estelle. Estelle, this is my friend and cook, Aoife."

Aoife placed the tea tray on the table between the two women and turned to Estelle. "You look like your mam."

"Yes, we've quite covered that." Adelaide added sugar and stirred her tea.

"I remember you as well. Cornsilk wisps all over your 'ead and so close to learnin' to crawl when Amber left town with ya." Aoife's gaze raked Estelle from head to toe.

"She preferred to be called Gilda." Estelle tilted her chin and met her gaze. She wouldn't be intimidated by these women. Well, she would, but she was determined not to let it show.

Adelaide calmly looked up from her tea. "So she did. Our apologies as well as our condolences on your loss. That will be all Aoife."

The cook's hard look softened. "Yes. Sorry for your loss. Your mam was a sweet gal." She nodded to her boss before turning to return to the kitchen.

Estelle picked up the dainty teacup, blew, then took

a sip, preferring it without sugar. She contemplated her words before speaking. She needed information and she wouldn't get it by taking offense to the woman's sharp tongue. Her mother spoke highly of Miss Adelaide and credited her with making sure she didn't end up on the streets. When her mother left Wylder for good, she assumed the last name, Adleton, in Adelaide's honor. "You don't seem surprised to see me."

She pinned her with a quelling look, as if trying to detect any sass in Estelle's tone. "I'd have had a short career if I allowed things to take me by surprise. A woman doesn't run a successful business in the west by being naïve."

Estelle resisted the urge to squirm and straightened her back. "I suppose you know why I'm here, then?"

"I have my suspicions, but I'd be a fool to show all my cards at once. What can I do for you, Estelle?"

Her mouth opened, then shut. She couldn't just blurt out that she wanted to know which men used to visit her mother.

"How about you tell me what you and your mother have been doing the last twenty-four years? I know she kept in touch with Mildred Lowery. Her letters to me were few before they stopped altogether, probably because I could never find the time to write back. I feel bad about that, but maintaining contact with me would not have helped her move forward. I cared for her and felt responsible for my husband's poor treatment of her, but at the end of the day, she was my husband's employee. We weren't friends." She placed her empty teacup on the tray and folded her hands in her lap.

Estelle tamped down her anger at the woman's disregard for her mother's feelings. "She always said you saved her life. She adopted a form of your name as our surname."

"I'm humbled by the honor she paid me by doing so. I simply introduced her to Mrs. Lowery and made a suggestion that solved problems for both of them. Nothing more. Now tell me about her life. What did your mother do with her opportunity to start over?"

"Mamma went to St. Paul to be a mail order bride for a rancher. He was older and ill when she arrived, so they planned to put the wedding off until he recovered, but he never did. He lingered on for another year and a half and just paid Mamma to cook and clean. When he finally passed, his estate went to a nephew, but he left Mamma a small sum that tide us over for a bit. After that, she answered an ad for Horton's Wild West Show."

Adelaide nodded. "That's about when I stopped hearing from her."

Estelle continued, "Tom Horton liked the look of her. He started her as an actress but had her start training to trick ride on the horses. When she was trained up, he billed her as Gilda the Gold and dressed her in gold clothes and feathers. She could ride standing on the saddle and she could make her horse do fancy steps."

"Tell me about your brother."

She'd better walk away with the information she came for. She hadn't had anyone to talk to about her mother in so long. Sharing Gilda's story served as a balm to her soul, but she still expected Adelaide's cooperation in the end. "Mamma took up with Ohanzee Cetan Wakuwa, a Lakota from the show. They never married. She birthed Wabli when I was seven." She didn't want to talk about Ohan, and Wabli's story was his own to share. She set her teacup next to Adelaide's and took a breath to steady her nerves. "I have a reason for coming to see you."

Adelaide relaxed back into her chair. "I assumed you did."

"I want to know who my father is." The clouds shifted in the sky and light poured into the room. *Illuminating it, how apt.*

The madam glanced at the window and raised an eyebrow before returning her gaze to Estelle. A faint smile crossed her lips but didn't reach her eyes. "You understand what we do here, don't you?"

Estelle nodded.

"I've made changes since my husband passed. It's safer for the girls, and we have a plentiful and varied clientele. I feel some degree of debt toward all the girls who worked for Farley. I couldn't help them then like I do now, and many suffered for it. But despite what I feel I owe them, I won't sacrifice my integrity to pay it. My livelihood and that of the girls living here depends on discretion." Adelaide rose and paced to the window.

Estelle braced her hands on the arms of the chair, unsure if she should stand or remain seated. "Do you know who he was? Mamma wrote about him. At least she wrote about one man in particular. She was fond of him and believed he fathered me. His name started with an *A*."

Adelaide looked over her shoulder at Estelle. "*A*, you say?" At Estelle's nod, she crossed to a tall cabinet. Using a key attached to her chatelaine, she unlocked it and opened the door. Inside, nearly identical bound books filled every shelf, reminding her of the one at the cavalry office. She reached for the top shelf and ran her fingers along the spines of the books shelved there.

"Eighteen fifty-two, eighteen fifty-three," she murmured, then pulled down the eighteen fifty-three volume. "When is your birthday?"

Estelle's hopes rose. "September of eighteen fifty-four."

"Hmm." She pulled down the eighteen fifty-four volume as well. She opened it and turned to the first page, running her finger down the paper. She closed it and put it back on the shelf. She repeated the gesture in the last few pages of the eighteen fifty-three volume before snapping it shut and replacing it as well.

Estelle rose. "Well, do you know who it is?"

Adelaide closed the cabinet and locked the door. She walked back to her chair and sat, placing her hands in her lap. She looked at Estelle. "No."

Estelle plopped back in her chair, causing Adelaide to frown. "But those were lists, a registry. You keep track of everyone that comes in here. My father's name must surely be there."

The madam held up her hand. "Perhaps."

"You might have an idea, but you won't share it." She nearly growled in frustration.

She tapped her index finger to her lips in a pondering gesture. "Tell me, Estelle, why do you want to know? What purpose would it serve to know the name of the man who accidentally fathered you while visiting a brothel? I don't mean to sound crass, but that is the truth of your conception."

Estelle huffed out a breath. How could she explain something she hadn't completely worked through herself? She wanted to see if her mother's thoughts had been fanciful. She wanted to decide if this man would have been worthy of her mother's esteem and protection.

Would he have been the father she always imagined?

"Mamma *loved* him. She didn't tell him about me because she didn't think he felt the same way and she wrote that he wasn't able to be a father to me or a husband to her. She thought it would be better to start fresh somewhere else. She didn't want the stigma of the choices she made and where I came from to stick to us. Even if my father claimed me, claimed us, the taint would always be there. She thought he was a good man and didn't want to burden him with that. I just want to see him—not even to meet him necessarily—but see what my mother saw."

Adelaide folder her hands neatly in her lap. "This is what I can do for you. Only two visitors during that time frame have names beginning with *A*. I don't know which one your mother was fascinated with; in my opinion, neither held much appeal. If you can discover the names on your own through alternative means, I will confirm or deny your suspicions. But you only get one chance. I'll only offer this compromise once. This will allow me to maintain the privacy of our customers, even though the incident occurred many years ago. Is this agreeable?"

"How am I supposed to do that? I know but one person in the whole town."

"From what I heard, you're already halfway to tracking down one of the gentlemen." The madam raised a slim eyebrow.

Estelle's cheeks heated at the memory of her embarrassing confrontation with Ezra. How in the world had Mrs. Willowby caught wind of it? She needed more evidence before she could present Ambrose Barlow's name to the madam. She couldn't waste her chance.

"Your *dear* auntie lived here at the time. I'm sure

the information is somewhere under that tight bun of hers. She'll have kept records of her customers, similar to mine. As the only seamstress in town, she had as many gentleman customers as I did, if not more." She smiled like a cat in cream.

Estelle heaved herself out of the chair. She could see why Aunt Millie warned her not to lower her guard around the woman. "I thank you for your time. It doesn't sound like you have anything more constructive to say, so I will take my leave."

Adelaide rose as well. "Oh poo. Don't be so sensitive. I've given you a solid place to start. Your aunt knows more than she realizes; you just need to help pry it out of her stubborn head." She followed Estelle to the door.

"I'll be back with a name." She glanced at the woman behind her.

"I do not doubt it for a moment," Adelaide said with a smirk.

****

With the sun directly overhead, Estelle arrived back at the white house. Surely its mistress would be awake by now. She hesitated briefly to consider the wisdom of calling during luncheon hours. But when the man of the house answers the door without shoes, it stands to reason the household doesn't stand on ceremony.

Her knock was again answered by Ezra, looking a good deal more groomed than the previous day. He'd shaved, exposing a dimple, wasted on such an unpleasant man. "You're back, Miss Adleton." He paused and gave her a knowing grin.

"I'd like to visit with your mother, if she's available." Estelle ignored whatever unspoken message he attempted to convey.

"Don't you want to know how I learnt your name?" His leer returned.

"Not particularly. Is Mrs. Barlow in?" Though she was a bit curious, not enough so to engage Ezra in further conversation.

"Ezra, who's at the door?" Una called from inside the house.

Ezra called over his shoulder. "It's Miss Adleton come back to see you."

"Well, don't leave her out on the porch for the neighbors to gawk at. Bring her into the parlor."

He turned back to Estelle, grin still in place. "You heard the woman, come on in. You and I can visit later." He stepped aside so she could pass through the doorway.

Estelle pressed as close to the edge as she could without being awkward, though her shoulder still grazed Ezra's chest. She suspected he moved toward her on purpose. He shut the door, cutting off the natural light, and directed her to a room at the end of the foyer on the right.

The house, so brilliantly white on the outside, was stuffy and dark on the inside. She again regretted not wearing the split skirt as she felt Ezra's gaze slither over her shoulders and down her trouser-clad legs. He laid a guiding hand on her arm to direct her into the parlor.

She jerked away. "I don't like to be touched."

He held both hands up in mock defense. "So you say…for now. My apologies."

Estelle strode ahead of him into the room. The drapes were open, allowing the sun to shine in on faded, once opulent furnishings.

Una sat in the middle of a green settee wearing a

lighter green dress that puffed up around her. She looked a bit like a frog on a lily pad. "Have you come to join my opposition team, to stop the school board? Ezra told me a woman stopped by yesterday. After he described you, I figured out who he was talking about."

Estelle stood next to a cushioned armchair, aware of Ezra hovering behind her. "Ah, no. I have a personal matter to discuss with you."

Una's lips formed a pout and her brow wrinkled in confusion. She beckoned her forward with a pudgy hand. "Come in, come in. Sit down."

Estelle started to sit in the closest chair.

"Not on the cushion, dear." Her frown deepened as she glanced at Estelle's trousers. "Ezra, bring that walnut armchair over here, please."

As soon as everyone was seated to Una's satisfaction, she turned her attention back to Estelle. "Are you here for Mildred? I can give you the information. I know she has to keep busy in her little shop to make a living."

"It's a matter regarding myself." Estelle's gaze flicked to Ezra, who sat in the cushioned chair. "A private, sensitive matter."

A shrewd look passed over Una's face. It seemed her curiosity for potential gossip had been piqued. "Ezra, be a dear and fix us a tea tray."

"We've just barely finished luncheon." He frowned.

"We have a guest. Go on now. Don't be rude." When they were at last alone, Una smiled at Estelle. "Do tell."

Estelle wished she'd spent more time planning what to say to the woman. She knew nothing of Una's relationship with Ambrose twenty-four years ago. She'd have to choose her words with care. "I am not only in town visiting my aunt." No need to mention Wabli's troubles if they haven't already hit the rumor mill. "I've come to find out who my father was."

Una tipped her head back and chortled, chins jiggling. "Oh, dear girl. You've set upon an impossible task. Don't you know what your mother was?"

Do not let your anger get away from you. You are about to give this woman bad news. She drew in a steadying breath. "I've been to see Mrs. Willowby. She will only confirm or deny the possibility of whatever names I present to her. She suggested speaking with discreet people who lived here at that time."

The woman puffed up her ample bosom with pride. "Of course, Addie sent you to me. There is no one more discreet."

Estelle pressed on. "My mother left a diary. She refers to the man she claims as my father by the letter *A*." She paused to see if Una would make the connection on her own.

Eyes bright, Una leaned forward, as if ready to feast on the juicy details. "That is not much to go on. I'll have to give it some thought."

"The only person Aunt Millie could think of, the only person the right age, was your husband. Ambrose. I'm sorry."

Una thumped back on the settee, face pale. "You're wrong. It could not have been him."

"I mean no disrespect, and I don't want to speak ill of the dead, but I want to find some answers. It's possible he may have gone to the Social Club when you attended evening meetings."

"No."

"I'm sorry, Mrs. Barlow. I know this is hurtful to you. Please, can we talk about the possibility Mr. Barlow may have been a customer of my mother's?"

She leaned forward again, glancing at the doorway. "You misunderstand me, girl," she said in a hissed whisper. "I know for a fact Ambrose was a regular visitor at that brothel. But there is no way he could be your father. No possible way."

Now Estelle frowned in confusion. "I know how things work. If he knew my mother in the biblical sense, he certainly could."

Another furtive glance at the doorway and another whispered reply. "Ambrose's male parts did not work while we were married. He was much older than I. Much older. We kept separate bedrooms and I refused to, ahem, entertain him."

This time Estelle's gaze slid to the doorway, and she whispered, "What about Ezra?"

"Ambrose is not Ezra's father." Her voice had dropped so low, Estelle could barely hear her. But someone else could.

A crash of porcelain and clatter of spoons sounded from the hall. Ezra stepped into the parlor with a haunted look on his face and a wet tea-colored stain down the front of his white slacks. Mother and son stared at each other.

Estelle rose with haste. "I'll see myself out. Thank you for your time. I'm sorry." She rambled the words out as she passed Ezra and scurried out of the room. Though she found both people unpleasant, destroying their little family had not been her intention.

Chapter 14

"Bring these to your brother," Mildred said gruffly as she thrust a brown paper wrapped parcel into Estelle's hands. "Don't make a fuss. They're just plain shortbread cookies. He looked thin when I saw him yesterday."

Estelle tempered her smile. "Of course, Auntie. I'm sure he'll enjoy them. The major is making sure he eats regular. He's probably just hit a growth spurt."

"Humph. Don't expect me to make more than two pairs of new britches for him if that happens. I'm a busy woman." Mildred accepted a brief hug from her niece.

"Thank you. For everything."

"Be off with you now. You're burnin' daylight and keeping me from my work." She made shooing motions as she circled her worktable. "I need to unlock the front."

"Have you thought of anyone else, any other men whose names start with an *A*? I think I've hit a dead end with Ambrose."

"Oh. Why is that? Did you speak with Una? She may not have liked it, but she'd a known what Ambrose was up to. She was a firecracker back in the day." Door unlocked and open sign flipped, Aunt Millie began pulling out cloth and placing it on the table.

"She knew, all right," Estelle said, then whispered, "Did you know Ezra isn't Ambrose's son?"

Her aunt's gray eyebrows flew up nearly to her hairline. "What's this?"

Estelle relayed what she had learned the previous day. "Did you have any idea?"

"At the time, no. But thinking back, Una and I were close friends then, I can't say I'm surprised."

This real-life drama tantalized Estelle. They may not be siblings, but she and poor Ezra had something in common. Neither knew who their fathers were. Though Ezra might by now. Estelle didn't stay to see how that situation panned out.

"Do you know who his father is?"

Mildred stared blankly for a moment, then blinked. "Not for sure, but I have a very strong suspicion. It's not good."

"Could the same person be my father?" Maybe she hadn't yet dodged the Ezra-brother bullet.

"Not likely. Besides, his name doesn't start with *A*."

"Will you tell me who it is?" Not that she would know the man from Adam.

"No good can come from it. Let it be." She pursed her lips together, ending the conversation.

****

Wabli worked alone in the cavalry office when Estelle stopped to visit. "Cookies! My favorite. Tell her thank you for me." He didn't take the time to unwrap the paper, instead sliced through it with his knife.

Estelle was glad to see Major Tucker, or just Tucker, as she'd began to think of him, had returned Wabli's belongings. He trusted her brother to work by himself, but that didn't mean he'd be safe in the office.

"I'll tell her, but you be sure to tell her yourself when she visits."

"It's strange. She knows all about me and I know all about her, but this week is the first we've met. She's a lot friendlier in her letters," Wabli mumbled around a mouthful of crumbs.

"She's kind. She just shows her love in a grumpy way. I don't think she gets close to many people." Similar to herself. All she needed was her brother and her aunt. Everyone else could stay at arms' length. Like the major. Her feelings about him were confusing. She needed his help with Wabli, and that's all. He could keep his gentle touches, solid arms, and his piney good smell to himself.

"Major Tucker said he'd wait for you at the livery when he finished his errands."

Estelle scowled. "I told him he doesn't need to ride out with me. I can take care of myself."

"I'm glad he is. I know you can handle yourself, Stella, but I'm afraid my father will find us eventually the longer I'm stuck here. I'm protected in the office, but you're not, especially outside of town. Don't be too mean to the major. Please?"

She snagged the last cookie before pulling Wabli into a hug. "I'll try."

****

Tucker waited for Estelle just outside the livery. Demon danced at the end of his tether and Starlight, already saddled, stood docilly at the rail.

"You must have a trustworthy face for Mr. Daniels to let you take my horse out." She greeted Star with a nose rub and a sugar cube from her pocket. Demon sidled over, eager for his share of attention and treats. She gave him a cube as well.

Tucker swung up into his saddle in one fluid motion while his horse was distracted. Once seated, he shrugged. "It's the uniform."

Estelle's gaze lingered on Tucker's solid back, the muscles shifting as he wrestled his horse into compliance. He cut an impressive figure; it certainly convinced her. Though that probably wasn't the same thing that convinced Chet Daniels.

This time they rode south of town past the stockyards and cemetery. The marker for the Barlow family plot could be read from the road. Estelle supposed that's where she'd find old Ambrose. Would it be worth the effort to poke around at the other headstones looking for *A* names? A shiver ran up her spine. Perhaps as a last resort. She'd forgotten to ask her aunt if she kept old ledgers from 1854. That could be her next step.

They finally let the horses run after crossing the bridge over the Medicine Bow River, Demon literally running circles around Starlight. When both horses had worked up a lather, the riders pointed them back toward the river.

"Since you won't share the secret you're keeping, will you tell me your plans for after your brother gains his freedom?"

"That's the question, isn't it? We left more abruptly than I'd planned. I have a little money saved, so does Wabli. We'd like to settle someplace permanently, maybe here, but I think we'll travel to some other places before we decide." How far and how long will depend on Wabli's father's determination to find them.

"Traveling is expensive. Do you have enough to do that and then purchase a homestead?"

Estelle frowned. She didn't need Tucker poking her loosely formed plan full of holes. "It's not really any of your business, is it."

"Wabli's a smart young man. He expressed interest

in doing something to help the Lakota people. I would assume that desire extends to other tribes as well. There are several ways he can do that, but they all start with furthering his education or apprenticing under someone in his interest field. Both of which point to living in a bigger city than Wylder or even Cheyenne."

What Tucker didn't say, is that it also meant money. Money to travel, money to buy a home, and money for her brother's education. Estelle wasn't trained to do anything but ride and shoot. No one would hire a woman for those things in the city. She was well-read and fair at sums. She could work at a shop or as a schoolteacher. Both of those things meant wearing a dress all the time. She scowled. "I don't have to decide today."

"No, but you probably best figure it out soon."

****

Tucker left Demon outside the livery while he helped Estelle untack and rub Starlight down. She didn't need the help but grudgingly admitted to not minding the company so much.

"How is the search for your father going?" He scooped a tin of grain from a barrel and dumped it in Star's trough.

She shrugged. "Not so well. My visit to the Social Club didn't turn up anything useful."

Tucker stilled. "Your visit where?"

"I went to see Adelaide Willowby, the owner of the Social Club. She knew my mother."

He moved into her space, close enough for Estelle to see fire in his blue eyes. "You went alone?"

She swallowed, then nodded.

He continued, "To a brothel, to see a madam? Are you out of your mind? Have you no sense whatever of your own safety?"

"My aunt knew where I went. She told me the safest time to go." She crossed her arms.

"Your aunt is a widow with a harsh tongue and prickly disposition. I don't imagine she strolls that way too often. If she did, her prominence in town would be enough to keep her safe. No one knows you. Someone could pluck you off the street and no one would know you were missing for hours." He motioned sharply with his hands as he talked.

Estelle fumed. How dare he yell at her? She fisted her hands at her sides and got in Tucker's face. "You seem to forget, I'm not that easy to pluck." She poked him in the chest.

He stepped closer, forcing her to look up at him. "You think so?" His voice deceptively quiet.

"I know so." She placed both hands on his chest, preparing to shove him out of her space. Anger simmered between them. Anger and something else equally intense. She braced herself. The last time she tried to shove him, he captured her wrists. This time she would follow through and put him against the wall.

That is not what happened next. Tucker's hands circled her wrists, as expected, but then he used her momentum against her and spun so her back hit the wall, arms splayed above her head. He easily held both wrists pinned to the wall with one large hand.

She could have escaped. Surprise and curiosity held her in place.

"Why won't you let anyone watch out for you?" he whispered before cradling the back of her head with his free hand and crushing his lips to hers.

In that instant, Estelle had no qualms about

surrendering control. The clouds of confusion from the past few days cleared and one defining word presented itself: desire. She desired this man like she had no other and returned his kiss with fervor.

She pulled a hand free, anxious to touch him. She ran her hand through his wavy hair, unresisted, his hat having fallen off with the first touch of his lips. He released her other hand and looped his arm around her waist, pulling her against him.

The noises of the livery barely registered in the background: Star's loud munching, a whinny from outside, footsteps.

"Major, come get your horse before he rips my rail down," Chet called from the front of the building.

Estelle emitted a small whimper when Tucker tore his lips from hers, cursing under his breath.

He still held her trapped against the wall but turned his head and called, "On my way." He turned back and released her waist, slowly untangling his fingers from her hair, never breaking eye contact. "That was…unplanned. I'm sorry."

Estelle narrowed her eyes at him. "I'm not. Go get your horse, Major." She ducked under his arm and slipped into the darkness of the stables to pay a visit to her brother's horse. They both needed time to process this new turn of events.

Chapter 15

Tucker cursed himself all the way back to the cavalry warehouse. For once, Demon's mercurial tendencies weren't a nuisance. Well, they were a nuisance, but the timing probably saved him from making a big mistake, an insurmountable one.

Estelle Adleton raised unfamiliar emotions within him. He'd never before felt desire as the other side of furiousness, yet she'd flipped them in him like a coin. He didn't toy with women. Ever. But this didn't feel like playing.

This felt dangerous. Maybe the wild oats he'd rarely sown in the past had come to a head. His body knew of his intentions to return to Boston and find a suitable wife. This was a final opportunity to indulge. But his head controlled his body, not the other way around. He'd never stoop to using Estelle or any other woman in such a manner.

He'd continue to keep an eye on her and make sure she didn't do anything to put herself in anymore danger, but no more kisses. No more heated conversations, and no more admiring her hair, and form, and spirit.

These things settled in is mind in time to force Demon toward the warehouse. His unruly mount reared, determined to return to the street. Odd, because the only thing that usually overruled the horse's obstinance was his stomach. Fresh oats awaited in yonder stall.

Then Tucker caught the scent Demon had already detected. Smoke. He jerked his head, trying to identify the source while remaining seated.

"Steady, friend. I smell it."

The office. Tucker saw smoke though the window but no flames. Wabli! He jumped from Demon's back.

"Stay! That's an order!" He'd deal with any insubordination later. His main concern was the young man in his charge.

He flung open the door. The fire smoldered inside a metal trash can, the flames long since dwindled. Leaving the door open, he rushed to open the windows.

"Wabli!"

"In here!" Came Wabli's voice from his room.

Guilt washed over Tucker. "Son, you're not really a prisoner. Why in the hell didn't you get help, or least get out?" He grabbed the doorknob.

"I couldn't. Captain Dooley locked me in." His voice cracked.

Tucker's heart broke at the terror in the boy's voice. He would have no idea the fire had been contained. Tucker grabbed the key from the desk and opened the door.

Wabli stood there, amongst stacks of books all over the floor, tears streaking down his cheeks. The boy dashed them away with his sleeve. "Is it out?"

"It is." A wet shirt had been rolled and laid at the base of the door. "Good thinking." Tucker nodded to it. "The fire was contained, but you still could have succumbed to the smoke. I'm sorry I left you for so long." *I'm sorry you almost died because I was too busy compromising your sister in the livery.* Tucker cursed himself inwardly. Estelle never would have forgiven him if Wabli got injured. He'd never forgive himself. "What happened?"

"The captain came in and yelled at me and said I was supposed to be locked up. I couldn't argue with him." His expression was bleak.

"I know, son. The best thing to do is just what you did. He might have been looking for a reason to hurt you." Tucker placed a reassuring hand on Wabli's shoulder. What happened next?

"I don't know. I heard him out there and then I smelled smoke. After I stuffed the door, I prayed." He shrugged.

"Let's go take a look."

All week he and Wabli had been working methodically through the stacks of invoices. Wabli wrote pages and pages of documentation in his precise script. Now, the desks were nearly bare.

"All my pages are gone," Wabli groaned. "It'll take forever to rewrite them."

"I think the bigger problem might be that the original invoices and all the evidence on them is gone, too." No evidence meant no charges. Sure, he could still court martial the man for a number of minor offenses, but the possible theft of fort supplies would be considered treasonous.

Wabli seemed to be quite recovered from his scare. A broad smile lit his face. "The ones I was working on were burned up as well as the months after that I hadn't started. So, only the last four months' worth of invoices are missing."

"There's a lot more missing than that." Tucker frowned.

"Come on." Wabli led Tucker back to his room. "I

knew you were planning to bind the invoices and receipts, so after I finished with them, I put them under the heavy books to flatten them back out. The older ones had been sitting a long time and were pretty curly. I'll have to write everything down again, but the source material is all here."

Tucker hooked an arm around Wabli's neck and mussed his hair. "Kid, you've just earned yourself a raise."

He freed himself and smoothed a hand over his locks. "You're not paying me."

"Extra desserts from Jake's?"

Wabli patted his belly. "With all the sitting I'm doing in here, my pants are getting tight."

Tucker grinned. "Then how about a ride?"

Wabli's face lit up. "Tonight?"

He shook his head. "No, I've still got to deal with a certain captain. How about tomorrow morning?"

"With Estelle?"

"Of course. While I'm gone, will you reorganize the papers left on the desks?" Wabli nodded and Tucker went to see a horse about a man.

****

"Sheriff!" Tucker hoped to find the man in an accommodating mood.

"Tarnation, Major. You don't have to yell." Sheriff Earl Hanson limped out from the back of the office.

Tucker removed his hat. "Apologies, sir. I'm in a bit of a tight spot. Seeing as I'm already housing a detainee in my offices, I don't have space for an actual prisoner. Do you have an open cell available until I can get some MPs out here to pick him up?"

"Well, I suppose that depends on who *him* is." Earl

scratched at his beard.

"Come see for yourself. It might be presumptuous on my part, but I think you'll find room for this one." Tucker opened the door so Earl could precede him out of the office. He tried to remain professional, but he couldn't keep humor from lacing his words.

"I'd be interested in hearin' this tale." Earl crossed his arms and leaned against the building, taking in the sight before him.

Demon was tied to the rail. One end of a rope was tied securely to the saddle pommel. The other end of the rope tied Captain Dooley's hands together. Demon had just enough leeway to nip at anyone daring to get close to his saddle.

Every attempt Dooley made to loosen the rope was met with either teeth or hooves, sometimes both. Tucker couldn't understand why the man hadn't given up.

Content to watch the show, Earl asked, "What'd he do?"

"Destroyed evidence. Set a fire in the office."

Earl turned to Tucker, frowning. "The kid all right?"

"Yes. It was contained and he locked Wabli in his room. Things could have gone wrong and ended badly, but we were lucky. Dooley was lucky. If anything had happened to the boy, I'd have killed him. No need for a trial."

Earl sighed. "Can't say I look forward to starin' at his ugly mug all day, but yeah, I'll take him for a couple days."

"If nothing else, this can only help Wabli's case."

Tucker untied Captain Dooley and led him next door to the jail and into a cell. "Don't give the sheriff any trouble, now."

Dooley sputtered. "I didn't do nuthin'. Why would you believe an injun kid over your own brother in arms? He's a liar. They're all liars."

"With a brother like you, who needs enemies. I'd trust that kid any day of the week before I'd turn my back to you." Tucker removed the rope and closed the cell door.

"It's his word over mine. Nothin's gonna come from this." He rubbed at the rope burns on his wrists.

"Maybe not, but it will give us enough time to compile all the evidence Wabli had in his room that didn't get burned. I bet something will come from that."

Dooley's face paled and he sat down heavily on the bunk.

"You have a good night, now." With that, Tucker nodded to the sheriff, returned his hat to his head, and strolled out of the jail.

Chapter 16

"Do we have to tell Stella about what happened?" Wabli walked beside Tucker who led Demon toward the livery.

"Don't you think we probably ought?" Tucker raised an eyebrow.

Wabli sighed. "Don't make a big fuss about it. The captain's locked up, so nothing like that can happen again. I don't know what she'll do if she doesn't trust that I'm safe there."

Tucker didn't know either. "I'll tell her you saved the day by hiding those invoices."

Wabli reddened. "Didn't hide them on purpose. Just lucky."

Tucker continued, "But the office still wreaks of smoke. If she comes by there, we'll have to explain in more detail."

"Good thing we're meeting her at the livery, then." The boy grinned.

After leaving the sheriff's office the previous afternoon, Tucker slid a note under the dress shop door inviting Estelle to ride with her brother the next morning. He'd dared not knock on her door and risk a repeat of their stable encounter. Besides, he stunk of smoke, too.

She'd agreed to the ride, via a note carried by Cecil when he brought breakfast an hour ago. So now, both he and Wabli in somewhat fresher-smelling clothes, headed to the livery to meet their fate.

"Thunder!" Wabli took off at a run to meet his horse, already saddled, waiting outside. Estelle and Starlight waited with him.

Wabli was on his horse before taking the time to greet his sister, which was for the best, she wouldn't have the opportunity to smell his clothing. Tucker let Wabli lead the telling of the event of the previous afternoon. "…and he locked me in my room and burned some papers in the trash can."

Estelle spun to glare at Tucker, who followed behind the siblings. "That could have turned into a dangerous situation. What happens if he tries to do it again while you're gone."

"Captain Dooley is keeping a room at the jail until someone from Fort Laramie comes to retrieve him," Tucker said.

She narrowed her eyes at him. "That sounds drastic for resecuring a detainee and burning a few papers."

Tucker resisted the urge to shift in his seat under her gaze. "There are extenuating circumstances. He attempted to burn evidence and he had no authority to lock Wabli in his room; I took over responsibility of your brother when I arrived. While I'm not prepared to file charges against him yet, I had him locked up for disobeying orders on principle. Also, he knows I'm looking closely at his dealings with the fort supplies. He was willing to risk punishment by his actions yesterday. That tells me he's a flight risk. Having him out of the barracks will also improve morale amongst the men."

"Hmm." She held his gaze for another moment before turning back around.

They rode till nearly noon, this time venturing to the

west of town. They returned to the livery and parted ways after taking care of Starlight and Thunder. Wabli helped care for Demon in the warehouse. After the long morning, Tucker hoped Cecil had left their meal in the office during their absence.

As they walked toward the office, a tall man in a brown greatcoat and bowler hat tied his horse to the rail out front, his collar turned up against the mid-November chill. Wabli stumbled.

Tucker steadied him with a hand to his elbow. When he returned his attention to the unexpected visitor, his own steps faltered.

The man dressed every bit the gentleman. The gap in his wool coat revealed a very proper, though worn, brown velvet vest underneath plaid jacket and matching trousers. The only concession to his debonair look were the leather Indian moccasins sticking out from beneath his cuffs. His footwear was the least surprising element making up, what Tucker believed to be, the most intimidating Indian he'd ever seen in his life.

"Hau, ahte. Hello, Father," Wabli said.

****

Why hadn't it occurred to Tucker to ask about Wabli's father? Knowing their mother's history, had he just assumed because Estelle was fatherless, Wabli would be as well? If he had given it due thought, he would have concluded that, had Wabli only been raised by his mother, he more than likely would have been named something like Joe or Tom. Tucker truly hated unforeseen complications. And this big Indian was going to be a problem.

The visitor said something to Wabli in Lakota. His resemblance to Wabli could not be denied. At seventeen, the boy already began to develop the sharp cheekbones and chiseled nose. The father's jowls and ruddy cheeks held the telltale signs of overindulgence in drink.

"No, Father. I can't leave," Wabli responded. "This is Major Tucker of the US Cavalry."

The Indian looked at Tucker. "I am Ohanzee Cetan Wakuwa, Wabli's father. I'm here to take him home."

Tucker placed a hand on Wabli's shoulder, causing Ohan to frown. "He's being detained on a criminal matter from before I arrived. I can't release him until the circuit judge arrives."

"I know your government's laws. He has not yet come of age. He is still considered my property and I can take him if I please." He crossed his arms, causing his biceps to bulge in his coat.

Tucker, tempted to mirror Ohan's stance, remained passive and kept a reassuring hand on the boy's shoulder. "That is true, but in this case, the crime is horse thieving, and he can be tried as an adult."

Ohan's brow rose and he glanced at his son. "You got caught stealing a horse?!" Tucker had a feeling the man was more upset about Wabli being caught than the alleged theft itself.

"No, Father. It is a misunderstanding, but I still have to be here when the judge comes," Wabli explained.

Ohan turned back to Tucker. "When will this be? The boy and I have responsibilities to return to. I've already taken enough time chasing after you. I've been to the livery and the sheriff's office. Where is Estelle?"

Tucker bristled at the proprietary way Ohan referred to Wabli's sister. Estelle was a full adult and no relation to him. She could come and go as she pleased.

"She's staying with Aunt Millie," Wabli supplied.

Ohan snorted. "You and Estelle have no family but me. This is a false relation. Where do I find her?"

Wabli opened his mouth to speak, but Tucker squeezed his shoulder.

"I'll let her know you're looking for her. She didn't mention that she expected anyone, and it wouldn't do for you to call on her unannounced. To answer your first question, the judge is delayed, but we expect him by the end of the week. Where are you staying?" Ohan was furious, that was certain, but the only visible signs were his deepening frown and a small tic at the corner of his eye.

"I do not know. My main concern was finding my son. Can you recommend a place where I would be welcome? If not, I will stay at the livery with my horse." Ohan's solicitousness sounded false to Tucker's ears, like a man used to telling people what they wanted to hear and doing whatever the hell he wanted anyway.

Tucker suspected Ohan used his gentleman's attire in a similar way, not that he could blame him. It hadn't helped Wabli but, generally, the more the Indians tried to blend, the easier time they had. Tucker wouldn't say they were accepted, but at least they were treated with less hostility and fear.

"Your money will be as good as anyone else's at the Wylder Hotel." He pointed north. "It's all the way at the other end of this road where it turns onto Wylder Street. You can't miss it." He could also get there without happening upon Lowery's.

"I will come see you tomorrow, Little Eagle. You will tell me what you and Estelle have been up to."

"Ha, ahte. Yes, Father," Wabli said as Ohan untied his mount and pointed him toward the livery.

When Ohan was out of earshot, Tucker turned to Wabli. "Is this the secret you and your sister have been keeping from me?"

Wabli cringed and cut his eyes to the side. "Yes, sir."

He should feel satisfied to finally know what he'd been missing. But it was too simple. The question he really wanted answered was why they left the wild west show in the first place. He wouldn't get that answer from Wabli tonight. Not when he suspected it was Estelle's secret to tell.

Chapter 17

Estelle stood uncomfortably at the bottom of the stairs of St. Joseph's Episcopal Church. She couldn't remember the last time she'd worn an actual skirt. Her own lone dress had been deemed unfit for church, and her aunt *just happened* to have a couple outfits in her size on hand. Thank goodness she'd been able to talk her aunt out of one with a bustle. She shuddered. The toes of her boots peeked out from under the hem. Her aunt didn't have anything that fit, so at least her feet wouldn't hurt.

"Come on. If we're not early, we're late." Her aunt waited midway up.

She sighed and her hand fought its way out from underneath the copious shawl, another acquiesce made to please Aunt Millie. She'd been forced to holster Flora to her leg for lack of inconspicuous pockets. She gripped the banister with one hand and clenched her skirt in the other and climbed the steps.

She remained close to her aunt as they mingled and greeted other early comers. "This is my niece, Estelle. Dear, this is Sally Smithers. We sit on a few church committees together."

"Welcome to Wylder, Estelle." Sally tapped her chin. "You look familiar."

Estelle recognized Sally as the woman who gave her terse directions to the livery when she arrived. Had it really been a week ago? "I saw you at the train station last Sunday afternoon."

Sally frowned. "Hmm. I don't recall, but then again, I was busy dealing with the mail order brides who came in on the train. Are you enjoying your visit?"

"For the most part, yes. I'm enjoying getting reacquainted with Aunt Millie." That's really the only part she'd truly enjoyed. She couldn't decide what category to put her encounters with the major in. Together with Wabli's troubles and the search for her father, her peace of mind was severely strained.

Mildred led Estelle to her usual pew, already occupied by her true niece, Sarah, and Sarah's new husband Daniel Taylor. She made introductions, explaining the Taylors owned a ranch and didn't make it into town very often.

The organ music began, and everyone quickly found seats. Estelle's party sat about midway back on the right side. In the front pew on her side, she recognized Finn Wylder from the mercantile and a few other familiar looking people.

Una and Ezra Barlow occupied the front pew on the left side. Una sat tall, gaze piously fixed on the pastor, except for the occasional elbow jab in Ezra's direction. Ezra constantly fidgeted and glanced over his shoulder around the sanctuary. When his eyes met Estelle's, he gave her a lecherous wink before returning to scanning the pews.

Estelle tried to focus on the sermon, but honestly, she found Ezra's strange behavior more intriguing. Finally, his gaze seemed to rest on someone seated a ways behind him. He settled and turned to face the front. Estelle decided he must have found who he searched for, because he barely twitched the rest of the service.

After the final blessing and dismissal, Ezra bolted from his pew and made a beeline toward the back. Estelle slowed her pace so she could see what had him in such a state. To her surprise, he approached Sally Smithers.

Ezra bent so he could talk to the much shorter woman. As he spoke, Mrs. Smithers' facial expression faded from politely condescending to bleak disbelief and anger.

"You, you, uncouth scalawag!" Sally lifted a hand, as if to slap Ezra, but then clasped it into a fist and shoved it into her shawl pocket.

Ezra wore a mystified, hurt expression.

Sally's gaze sought and found Una, who had paused to chat with a group of ladies. "And you!" She yelled across the room. "You couldn't let it rest. My Robert's dead and gone and you still had to go and rip open the wound of my greatest humiliation. You horrible, awful woman!" She let out a frustrated cry and rushed out of the building.

A hush fell over the remaining congregation, of which there were quite a few. Una's pouty mouth had popped open in surprise during Sally's tirade. She closed it now, her teeth making a small click. She flushed from the top of her low-cut neckline all the way to the graying roots of her blonde hair.

"Excuse me," she choked out to her little group. She bustled up the aisle and grabbed Ezra by his elbow. "Let's go," she hissed. She had many more whispered words for her son, but none that Estelle could make out.

Next to her, Aunt Millie sighed. "No good at all."

"What just happened?"

"Una's had a comeuppance. Her misdeeds are exposed, to the mortification of poor Sally."

Estelle put the puzzle pieces together in her mind. Sally's late husband, Robert, must be Ezra's father. Robert and Una were both unfaithful to their spouses.

"This is all my fault." Estelle's probing hurt innocent and not-so-innocent people.

"No. Poor Sally did more damage to her reputation with her emotional outburst. No one will remember in a couple weeks. I only understand what happened because of what you told me and my friendship with both women years ago. I'm sure Sally knew back then, or at least suspected. The person to feel sad for is Ezra."

"I'm not inclined to feel sorry for Ezra." Estelle wrinkled her nose remembering the wink.

"Robert Smithers, for the most part, was a good man who made one mistake. Sally is barren and had a hard time coming to terms with it. Robert was weak, and when things weren't so happy at home, allowed himself to be seduced by a serpent. None of this is your doing. There's no need to carry any guilt over it." Her aunt patted her on the arm and made her way to the back of the church where the pastor greeted folks as they left.

The low whistle of the train coming into town echoed in her heart and she decided maybe she did feel a little bad for that numbskull Ezra.

****

"Stella! You look like a lady." Wabli's cheeks flushed.

"The church service this morning was a disaster, not the service, but after. I wanted to come see you before going home to change. As soon as I'm in my regular duds, Star and I are riding hard." She fussed with the shawl until both hands were free and she could hug her brother.

"Stell, something happened." Wabli's tone was grave.

"What? Did Dooley come back? Where is Major Tucker?"

"He went to the telegraph office. He'll be right back. Listen."

She stilled.

"Father is here."

Estelle stepped back and fell into a chair. Had it not been there, she would have ended up on the floor and probably not noticed. Her mind immediately began jumping four, five, ten paces ahead. Curse that judge and his gouty foot! She and Wabli should have been prairies and towns away by now. She suddenly realized Wabli was still speaking.

"…at the Wylder Hotel. He wanted to take me back, and you too, I think, but the major wouldn't let him."

"If he takes you, I'll go with you. We'll leave again when you turn eighteen."

"If you go back Horton will make you sign a contract. Otherwise, you won't be able to travel with us. Then you'll be stuck." His voice laced with shame and worry. No matter how many times she told him; he wouldn't believe her problems weren't his fault. They looked out for each other. They'd both made that promise to Mama.

"I'll worry about it when and if it comes. Is he coming back to see you today?"

Wabli glanced nervously out the windows. "He said he'd come this morning, but I haven't seen him yet."

"I don't want him to find me here. I'll have to face him eventually, but I'm going to put it off as long as I can. He's going to blame me for your runnin' off."

Finally, Wabli offered a half-smile. "I suppose it was kind of your fault."

Estelle punched him in the arm, gave him another hug, and hurried home to change for her ride, eyes peeled for the man of her nightmares.

Chapter 18

Estelle hurried from the dress shop to the livery as fast as she could while still appearing proper. She had to determine all of the possible ramifications of Ohan being in Wylder. The best place to sort out her thoughts was on the back of her horse. She'd changed into her split skirt and fringed coat after visiting her brother. Flora, no longer holstered to her leg, now provided a comforting weight to her pocket.

She slipped into the livery. Star whickered a greeting.

"Hello, sweet girl. I'm sorry I forgot your sugar." Estelle rubbed Star's neck and back. She placed a saddle blanket on the horse's back, then lifted her saddle from its stand and put it on top. She stooped to reach under Star for the front cinch strap.

Star whinnied and side-stepped as a strong arm wrapped around Estelle's torso and pulled her out of the stall.

"Be still woman." The voice of her nightmares commanded.

Estelle stifled a scream, not wanting to panic all the livestock. She did try to grab on to corners and stall doors as Ohan dragged her to the depths of the livery. Her fingers failed to find purchase, though she came away with several splinters that would require attention later.

Ohan brought her to a room way in the back she

hadn't known existed. A narrow workbench lined one wall and worn, or broken tack hung on the opposite one. A small window allowed enough natural light to see clearly. He shut the door and, failing to find a locking mechanism, leaned back against it. Ohan's arm still pinned her to his front.

"We have much to talk about, woman. You have forgotten your place and tried to turn my son from me." His mouth was too close to her ear for her liking.

She struggled against his hold, too far away from anything that could be used as a weapon. His arm pinned her pocket closed, cutting off her access to Flora. "Wabli left and I followed him."

"Had you stayed, we could have searched for him together."

"I don't want to be anywhere near you or do anything *together* with you. I never intended to stay."

"Our time of mourning your mother is passed. It is time to take your mother's place at my side and in my bed." His free hand caressed her cheek then dropped to her breast, thankfully covered by clothing layers and her coat. Ohan's touch again evoked the memory her dreaming self wouldn't let her forget.

The hand moved from her back and slid to her breast, squeezing it through her night dress. She bit her lip to keep from screaming. If he thought she slept, he might leave. Though no one would be able to sleep through such rough handling.

She opened her eyes, hoping to see hints of dawn creeping through the flaps of the tent. Daylight meant people and activity. It was still too dark to see the brown canvas wall in front of her face. The hand slipped under the blanket and glided down her stomach and hip. The

120

fingers pinched the hem of her nightgown and began to tow it up her leg.

A tear leaked from her eye. He'd be furious and she'd have to leave Horton's at once but pretending to sleep wasn't working this time. She took a deep breath to scream, but a hand clamped over her mouth. Ohan's leg came down, pinning hers, when she struggled.

He whispered something in Lakota as his hand made its way upward on her bare skin.

"Father." Wabli's voice, sounding older than his years, penetrated the darkness.

Ohan answered in Lakota.

"No." Solid. Sure. "Stella, are you all right?"

Ohan responded again.

Wabli ignored him. "Stella, answer me."

The hand came away from her mouth, but the other squeezed her skin lightly, a threat of worse to come. She sucked in air around a sob. "I, I need to go to the outhouse," she whispered.

"I'll walk with you. That's where I was heading. Father, I noticed you were gone. Did you mistake this tent for ours?" Wabli asked in an even tone.

Ohan grunted a response and slowly untangled himself from Estelle.

Estelle listened as he shuffled across the darkened tent. When she heard the flap fall back into place, she sat up.

Wabli sat down next to her and put an arm around her shoulders. She wrapped both arms around him and sobbed into his chest. He sat with her until dawn and the next night slept on a pallet across from her camp bed.

Estelle stilled. His actions made it clear he wanted her to take her mother's place in his bed, but he'd never voiced his desire to fulfil her place in all ways. The thought of such a farce made her ill. "That won't happen. I'm not returning to Horton's."

"You will come for your brother." A smirk laced his voice. "The laws of your own people say he is mine until he is eighteen."

Enough of this. Estelle brought her foot down on his instep. His moccasins no match for her heeled boots, he cursed as she spun away. She put her back against the opposite wall and wrapped her hand around Flora. When Ohan lurched toward her, she pointed the gun at his chest.

****

"What took you so long?!"

Tucker returned to the cavalry office to find Wabli pacing the floor. "I saw Sheriff Hanson while I was there and owed it to him to listen to him complain about the captain. Good news, though—"

"It can wait. I'm worried about Stella."

"What's wrong?" He removed his hat but didn't hang it up. Whatever the trouble, it wasn't at the office.

"My father said he'd come see me this morning, but he hasn't come yet."

"And?" The boy usually wasn't one for theatrics.

"Stella came by after church. I told her about Ohan. She said she was going to go riding."

Tucker still didn't understand the urgency. He grabbed Wabli by the shoulders to hold him still and looked him the eyes. "If your sister is in some kind of trouble beyond the usual foolhardiness of riding out alone, you need to say it right now."

Wabli cut his eyes to the side. "She doesn't like my father."

"*I* don't much care for your father either. What else?"

"My father likes her. A lot." He still wouldn't meet Tucker's gaze.

Tucker puzzled it for a moment and gave Wabli a little shake. "Did he hurt her?"

Finally, he raised his eyes. "He tried to. That's why I left, to get him to come after me and leave her alone."

"To Chicago?"

Wabli nodded. "But I made it worse. I'm stuck in here and I can't protect her."

Tucker cursed and slammed his hat back on his head. "Stay here." He bolted out the door.

****

His intention upon returning from his errand had been to take Wabli out riding again, so he'd saddled Demon in preparation. He untied the reigns and mounted, turning the horse around before he had both feet in the stirrups.

Demon took off toward the livery and soon Tucker could see Ohan's horse tied out front. His boots hit the dirt with a thud, and he secured Demon to a different rail. He rushed inside, but no damsel in distress awaited him. He approached Starlight's stall, and she whickered a greeting.

The horse's saddle was in place, but not buckled. He picked up Estelle's hat from the floor and cursed. Backing out of the stall, he searched the space. Disturbed straw and drag marks leading to the back drew his attention.

The door to the repair room was closed. Tucker crept to the door to listen.

"You point a gun at me, Gilda?"

"That's not my name. Let me out."

"You look just like her. You and Wabli will come back with me, and you can take your mother's place in the show. You need me to help you. You will understand in time. I gave you time to grieve and you repaid me by taking my son and leaving. My patience has run out. You will return with me to the hotel and stay there until the trouble with Wabli is over."

"No. You will let me out and I will go about my business. You will leave me alone." Estelle's voice held a slight tremor. Tucker's anger at the deluded man spiked. He wanted to rush in, be he needed to fully understand the situation first, especially if Estelle pointed a gun at Ohan.

"Then I will take my son and you will never see him again."

"He'll leave when he turns eighteen anyway."

"By then I will have turned him against you."

If Ohan weren't so big and dangerous, Tucker would have laughed at his naivety. Or perhaps drink had so affected his mind he believed he had a real way to control his son.

"Stay away from me. Don't think I won't shoot you."

"Gilda…" Ohan's voice wasn't next to the door anymore.

Tucker put his shoulder to the door and shoved. Ohan had only taken one step away, so the edge of the door hit him in the middle of the back, causing him to stumble. Estelle screamed and put her hands out defensively. Tucker suspected skill and training were the only things that prevented her from accidently pulling the trigger.

Tucker tackled Ohan to the ground placed a knee on his back. Estelle knelt and pushed the gun barrel into Ohan's temple. Though her finger remained off the trigger, the threat was effective.

"I have this handled. Go see your brother, he's worried sick."

She seemed hesitant to move. "What are you going to do?"

"We're going to go visit the sheriff and encroach upon the town's accommodations one more time."

Chet Daniels appeared in the doorway, out of breath. "What the hell's goin' on, Major?"

"I need to make a trip to the sheriff's office. Do you have a wagon I can borrow for an hour or so?"

Daniels looked from Estelle to Tucker to the subdued man on the floor. "Are you all right, ma'am?"

Estelle rose and brushed off her skirt. It was the split one that intrigued him so. She slipped her little gun into her coat pocket. "I've decided not to ride after all, Mr. Daniels. I'll go put Star's saddle away." She stepped around the men on the floor.

"Miss Adleton." Now that she was safe, Tucker's frustration at the siblings' secret turned to fury at the situation it'd caused. She'd misled him regarding the circumstances surrounding her brother. He'd trusted her, but she hadn't been able to do the same.

She paused. "Yes?"

"We *will* discuss this later."

She nodded, apprehension in her eyes, then left.

125

Chapter 19

Of course, Estelle was long gone by the time Tucker made it back to the cavalry office late Sunday afternoon. He spoke briefly with Wabli and answered questions about details his sister had refused to share. She needed to stop babying him.

Tucker went to bed angry and woke up surly. He and Wabli had been working all morning, finally binding the papers into account books.

"Are you mad at me?" Wabli asked.

Tucker looked up from his work. "No, why do you ask?"

"I can tell you're in a bad mood. Stella said something last night about you being angry at her. Are you?"

Tucker leaned back in his chair. "That's between me and your sister."

"I didn't tell you about my father, either. You should be mad at me, too." The boy was astute, Tucker would give him that.

Tucker dragged his hand down his face. He didn't feel like dissecting his feelings for Estelle with her little brother. But he and the boy had developed a friendly relationship, maybe talking to someone would help. Not in detail, of course.

"You were keeping a confidence for her. You were right in that, mostly. It was her story to tell. She's an adult, and as such should have given me all the information I needed to keep you both safe. Even a warning that the man might come looking for you would have been helpful." Tucker sighed. "There's nothing more to be done about it. The time for you to tell me was Saturday night when your father arrived. I would have been on the alert to watch out for your sister. So no, I'm not mad at you. You made a mistake and hopefully learned a lesson about when to share information and when to keep it."

Wabli nodded thoughtfully. "Then why are you still mad at Stella?"

"That's a trust issue. She didn't trust me, even though she told me there was nothing else I needed to know. I knew she hid a secret, but I assumed it didn't involve your situation. Even though I gave her plenty of opportunity, she never shared she might be in danger."

"Oh. Trust is important in a relationship."

"What? I don't have a relationship with your sister." Had he let any of his feelings show?

"You're friends with her, right?"

He hesitated, unsure. "Possibly."

Wabli rolled his eyes. "You and I are friends, aren't we?"

"I'd like to think so."

"So it's important that we trust each other. I won't withhold information ever again." He stood and held his hand out solemnly to Tucker.

Tucker didn't know what kind of role models Wabli had in his life besides his father, but he felt humbled and honored that the boy seemed to consider him as such. He shook Wabli's outstretched hand. "I promise to be honorable in my dealings with you, as well."

Wabli nodded and sat back down. "What about Stella?"

"That is between me and your sister."

Tucker's fury abated but his feeling were still unsettled. He wasn't so much angry as…hurt? And maybe a little embarrassed that he lent his own trust so easily. Estelle claimed again and again that she didn't need anyone. Tucker played the fool by not believing her. She didn't need him. She didn't feel anything for him.

After working quietly for a while, Wabli paused. "What news?"

Tucker looked up from his task. "Pardon?"

"When you came back yesterday, before you left to rescue Stella—"

"She didn't need rescuing, though I may have saved your father's life."

Wabli waved him off. "The last thing you said was *Great news*."

Tucker replayed the day in his head. "Oh! Yes, the wire office had a message for me, several actually. I heard from my friend at Fort Laramie, and he said shipments are usually off. Sometimes over, but mostly short. The other fort reported similar problems, but never enough to make it worth the time to pursue. They were short what had been ordered, but the invoices were usually accurate."

"That doesn't sound like *great* news."

"I also received a separate wire from a sergeant at Fort Russell. He'd been investigating the soldier who handles their receivables. He intercepted a letter from Captain Dooley."

"What did it say?" Wabli's eyes lit up.

"I don't know. The sergeant told me to watch for a letter soon. I imagine there was too much detail to get into over telegraph. But it's enough to justify sending for the military police to escort Captain Dooley to Fort Laramie. And enough for me to write a nomination for you for a civilian service award." Tucker smiled, Wabli's enthusiasm pulling him out of his dark mood.

"Really? I don't know what that is, but it sounds important."

"It is. And it will help you with whatever you decide to do in life."

"It feels good."

"What does?"

"Putting things right, helping bring about justice. Maybe I could be an attorney, like you, or a Pinkerton agent." He looked thoughtful. "Which one do you think would help the Lakota people more?"

"It depends. As an agent, you'd go where they send you to investigate a case. As an attorney, you'd have the potential for more autonomy. You could practice where your people need you most, whether it be locally or in Washington." Maybe this is how Tucker could also assuage some of the guilt he felt over how the U.S. Government treated the native population. He could mentor Wabli, sponsor his schooling, and set him on a path to advocate for his people. "Give it some thought. I'll answer whatever questions you have."

****

Estelle slipped into the cavalry office late in the afternoon. She'd hoped Tucker would be out doing soldiering things and she could visit with Wabli in peace. Peace being relative. What she really wanted was to postpone the unavoidable conversation he wanted to have.

Why hadn't she trusted Tucker? She didn't want to think or talk about Ohan. Speak of the devil and he shall appear. It didn't matter in the end. Her own personal demon tracked her down anyway, scary as ever and crazy as a Bessie bug.

Ohan had crawled into her bed, made her feel powerless. Telling Tucker those things would be admitting she truly couldn't take care of herself in all circumstances. She refused to expose her weaknesses to anyone. Weak women gave up control, gave up their power.

Her mother was strong enough to break free of prostitution and make a life for herself. Then, she'd saved her money and planned to free herself from the wild west show so she could give her daughter a normal life. But Ohan came along, and she became weak for him. Wabli was the only good to come from their entanglement.

Wabli looked up and his expression brightened. "Stella! Guess what. I'm thinking about being a lawyer like Major Tucker so I can help the Lakota."

She glared at Tucker, all trepidation forgotten. "What are you fillin' his head with?"

Tucker rose when she entered the office. He returned her glare. "You know how smart your brother is. I've offered to sponsor him when he passes the entrance exams."

"Nice of you to talk to me about it first."

"Stella, I want to do this." Wabli had also risen and moved to stand next to her.

"You would hold him back?" Tucker asked.

"No! He's my brother. You can't go making plans

and decisions behind my back."

"It was *never my* intention to keep *anything* from you." Tucker's sarcasm leaded voice hit Estelle like a mule kick.

"I think I'd better go. Wabli, I'll come by tomorrow." She gave her brother a hug and turned to the door.

"I'll walk with you." Tucker walked around the desk and took his greatcoat from its hook.

"I'd rather you didn't."

"I'd rather you not argue with me about something that's going to happen whether you like it or not." He opened the door and turned to Wabli. "I'll be right back."

"Stella, please," Wabli pleaded behind her.

"Goodnight, Little Eagle." She went out into the dusky evening. Tucker fell into step beside her.

"I'm so angry with you," he said.

"Well, the feeling is mutual, now. How dare you deal with my brother without me present." She had her hands shoved deep in her pockets to ward off the chill.

"You know that wasn't my intention. We were having a conversation and I answered his questions. He's going to be a man soon and have to make decisions as a man. He won't get far trailing on your apron strings."

She scowled. "How dare you. You know nothing of our relationship."

"Wabli and I are friends. Do you realize how upset he is about everything that happened with his father? Because you refused to tell me and share the burden, your brother felt the full responsibility of your safety rested on his narrow shoulders. Because Ohan is his father, he felt doubly responsible. Was that your intention?" Tucker never raised his voice, but his words cut, nonetheless.

"I'm responsible for him," she whispered.

"That, my dear, is not how honorable men are built. And your brother is on his way to being a very honorable man." He paused. When he spoke again the edge in his tone was gone. "It's not how I'm built, either. When I thought you were in danger, it crushed me. Then finding out your own actions prevented me from protecting you…" He seemed to struggle for the word. "Hurt. It hurt. You see, I thought we were becoming friends, too."

She opened her mouth to speak, but no words came.

Tucker glanced up at her door. "You're here. Have a good night, Estelle." He left without a kiss or even a touch. She found she missed those things from him very much.

Chapter 20

Estelle and Tucker managed to avoid each other most of the week. When she stopped to visit Wabli, the major would leave to run an errand. It didn't matter though. Her conversations with her brother consisted of 'the major said this' and 'the major suggested that'. She couldn't escape thinking of the man.

He disturbed her sleep every night in her dreams. While preferable to the nightmares of Ohan, they made her just as restless. How had she grown so accustomed to a man in such a brief amount of time?

She trudged back to the dress shop Thursday afternoon. Her aunt waited outside with a shawl wrapped around her shoulders. Estelle greeted her with a weary smile.

"Tea's ready. Come in and sit," Mildred ordered.

"I'd rather go up to my room and rest for a bit."

"Don't care." She opened the door and went in leaving Estelle no choice but to follow.

Once seated, her aunt handed her a cup. "No sugar, I remember." She settled back in her chair and took a sip. "Mmm, perfect." Then she turned her gaze to Estelle. "What do you plan to do with your life?"

Estelle sputtered. "Aren't we supposed to chat about the weather and the price of flour before you ask the heavy questions?"

"Nope. I either already know or don't care about

those things. So, I'm starting with what I don't know and do care about. Saves time that way." Sip.

Maybe talking to her aunt would help her work out the answers for herself. "I'd always planned to leave Horton's. I wanted a homestead and maybe some animals. I thought Wabli would want to run it with me."

"He's a young man. He'll have his own oats to sow and not want to be weighed down by a spinster sister."

She cringed at her aunt's blunt but no less truthful statement. "He wants to be a lawyer so he can help the Lakota."

"Hmph. Lord knows they need someone smart on their side. I suppose that's a noble calling. Better than horse racing and pretending to take scalps." Her aunt grimaced.

"Where does that leave me?"

"You're not his responsibility, and in several months, he won't be yours. You need a new plan, girly." She said this kindly.

Estelle looked around the shop. "You're by yourself, and you've managed to run a successful business for a long time. I could do something like that, run a shop, but not sewing."

"Hmph. I've heard about your failed stitching exploits." Mildred's lips were pursed but Estelle sensed her aunt fought a smirk.

"I don't know how to do anything a woman's supposed to know how to do."

"Listen here. I've been lucky. I'm the only seamstress and wash house in town. It's not my pretty face or my sunny disposition that keeps bringing folks back, just good old-fashioned necessity and laziness.

"Another reason is Horace. He left me enough funds

to carry me through a few lean times. Plus, folks around here look out for each other. Race had good friends in this town. It would shame them to see a friend's widow fall on ruin. So, you see, there are a lot of things working for me in Wylder. I couldn't leave and be as successful anyplace else." She set her empty teacup down and rested her hands in her lap. "You may not think you need anyone to help you, but it sure is nice to have someone around." Her gaze lingered on the door that used to be Horace's clock workshop. "Like your Major Tucker."

"He's not my Major Tucker." *He may have almost been, but not anymore.* "I thought about moving to wherever Wabli goes to school. I can find a job." She perked up. "I could work at a livery."

"Ha! Not likely." Mildred slapped her knee. "Your brother will end up going east for schooling. You won't get far past the Mississippi River in your trousers and trapper's coat before they send you packing back to the heathen west."

The dress shop door flew open, and Cecil stood on the stoop. "The judge is here. The major sent me to fetch ya to the sheriff's office."

Mildred stood. "Consider us fetched, young man. Now shut that door, I'm not heating the whole town."

****

When they arrived at the sheriff's office, Earl Hanson escorted them down the street to the doctor's office. "He's only just recovered. Doc Sullivan's giving him a treatment." Estelle found it odd that the judge agreed to see them while indisposed, but she attributed it to small town eccentricities.

A handsome man with long hair greeted them at the door and showed them to a room in the back where the judge sat in a chair, foot propped on a stool. Major Tucker and Wabli stood by a window and Captain Dooley sat in a chair next to them looking a little worse for wear.

Estelle was glad to see Wabli dressed in the new pants and shirt Aunt Millie made him. Seeing him in clothes properly fitted drove home her aunt's comments about Wabli becoming a man. Though only simple shirt and trousers, he looked like a respectable man about town. It made her sad.

"We've got quite a party, I see. My apologies, Doc. I didn't realize this case would be such a big to do," the judge said.

"No trouble at all. I'm going out for a bit. Send someone to the mercantile for me if you need anything." The doctor left, closing the door behind him.

"I'm Judge Read. I apologize to you folks as well. I don't like to let cases on my docket draw out for so long, but circumstances couldn't be helped." He gestured at his unshod foot resting on the stool, covered with a white towel. "So, let's get this ball rolling, shall we?" He pulled a telegraph message out of a satchel by his chair. "Says here, the charge is horse thievin'." He looked at the assembled group over the rim of his spectacles. "Sheriff, why don't you fill me in before I take statements."

Earl cleared his throat and stepped forward. "I contacted you on behalf of the cavalry office. The captain here, arrested the young man, and has kept him in custody at their office. I'm here as a representative of the town and to return the prisoner to my jail when we're through."

"Unless I release him, that is," the judge said.

Earl coughed. "Well, no. The prisoner I'm referring to isn't on trial today. We've been referring to Wabli," he jerked his head in Wabli's direction. "As a detainee."

"I wasn't aware of a second case."

"This one's a military matter, but they didn't have no place to put him until the military police come get him," Earl explained.

The judge scrubbed a hand down his face. "Let me get this straight. The horse thief has been locked up at the cavalry office while a military prisoner is in your jail?"

"Yep. That about sums it up." The sheriff leaned back against the wall; his part done.

"Who arrested the horse thief?" He looked over at Tucker and the captain.

"I did Your Honor." Dooley began to rise, but Tucker forced him back in his seat with a hand to the shoulder.

Judge Read focused on Tucker. "And who are you?"

"Major James Tucker, Your Honor. Colonel Egar sent me from Fort Laramie to assess the situation and take care of some other problems reported about the Wylder office."

"Mmm. Egar. Good man; been a long time," Read mumbled mostly to himself. "And what was your assessment, Major?"

"My assessment of this particular case it that Captain Dooley wasted your time by requesting your presence. The alleged thief is the owner of the horse he is accused of stealing."

"Then why in tarnation didn't you cancel my summons?" Read sputtered.

"You were already enroute by the time I arrived.

Since the process had already been initiated, the case could not be dismissed until proper protocol had been fulfilled."

Read snorted. "What are you, some kind of lawyer?"

Tucker smirked. "Something like that, yes, Your Honor."

Read eyed him speculatively. "All right then, case dismissed. I'd be darn mad if this hadn't been so all fired entertaining. Now, tell me, who is the good sheriff's prisoner?"

Estelle's heart thumped with relief. It was all she could do to keep from grinning like a madwoman and dancing a jig.

Tucker glanced at the captain who hung his head.

The judge slapped his thigh and grimaced when the foot attached shifted. "Doggone, this is the first time I've arrived to a town to find the accuser locked up and the accused already exonerated. I can retire a happy man. Indulge me, if you would. What'd he do?"

The captain scowled as Tucker answered. "Skimming, inventory theft."

Nodding, Read turned to Mildred and Estelle. "Ladies, seems like I'm plum full of apologies this afternoon. This little trial got away from me before we got to the niceties." He beckoned the ladies forward and took Mildred's hand. "And you are?" He brought her hand to his lips and deposited a quick kiss.

Mildred blushed furiously. "I'm Mildred Lowery, aunt of the accused." She bobbed a half curtsey. "Your Honor."

Estelle stared agog at her normally grouchy, aunt's behavior. She flinched, surprised when the judge took her hand next. "And you, miss?" Thankfully he forewent the kiss.

"Wabli is my brother, sir, Your Honor." The instinct to perform her own curtsey was surprisingly strong, but she stiffened her spine. The man wasn't royalty, for goodness sake.

He released her hand and turned to Wabli. "Young man, come over here."

Wabli moved to the spot next to Estelle and offered his right hand. "Hello, Your Honor. Thank you for coming."

Pride bubbled up inside Estelle's chest.

Read accepted Wabli's hand and pumped it firmly. "Young man, are you aware of the circumstances that got you into this predicament?"

He nodded. "I am, Your Honor."

"More'n likely, this isn't the last time you'll find yourself dealing with trouble through no fault of your own. I don't have a solution to that, only advice. Stay clean, educate yourself, and be vigilant. It may help you steer clear of at least half the trouble your kind faces out there." He turned to Earl. "We're done here, Sheriff. You can take your prisoner."

Earl pulled the captain to his feet and took his leave. Tucker gestured for the ladies to precede him out.

"Hold up a minute, Major. You can escort me to my rooms at the Wylder Hotel and catch me up on what ol' Ernie Egar's doing these days."

"It would be my pleasure, Your Honor."

Read chuckled. "You sat that now, but you'll probably be supportin' most of my weight by the time we get there. Ladies, it was a delight to meet you both."

"Thank you, Your Honor. I hope you get to feelin' better," Estelle said. With Tucker occupied, there was nothing left to do but leave with her little family.

Chapter 21

Estelle shouldn't have been surprised when Tucker failed to come see her after helping Judge Read. It didn't make it hurt any less and didn't keep her from continuing to be confused over her emotions. He'd made it clear there would be no more close encounters between them. Nothing kept her from knocking the dust from her boots and moving on.

Of course, that wasn't exactly true. He planned to mentor Wabli. He'd be a part of her brother's life and, by extension, her own. Especially if she planned to live near Wabli's school. She'd know when Tucker found the perfect woman to marry and when he became a father to that perfect woman's children. Estelle's stomach churned.

After a restless night, and needing an escape from her torturous thoughts, she sought her aunt's company in the dress shop. Wabli kept his room at the cavalry office since it offered him a bit of privacy compared to taking a pallet in Estelle's room. Besides, he still had the job to complete with the major, her brother had reported with pride.

"Will you teach me to sew, Auntie? Maybe my problem had more to do with the teacher instead of the student."

Mildred looked up from her work. "I doubt that. Your mother had a little skill when I met her. I helped her refine it. She wrote you never wanted to sit still for a lesson. I doubt much has changed."

"So, you won't teach me?"

"No point. You know the basics, just takes practice. Why do you ask, anyway?"

Estelle fidgeted, lending evidence to her mother's complaint. "I'm tryin' to find a way to support myself when I leave with Wabli."

Her aunt set down her scissors and began pinning seams together. "Maybe you should find a job where you poke your nose in other people's business."

"Auntie! I do not do that." Did her aunt really think so little of her?

"You did, but not to anyone who didn't deserve pokin'. 'Cept Sally, of course." She continued working as if her statements hadn't been unforgivably rude. "Maybe a reporter or something," she added.

"I didn't mean to stir up a hornet's nest. I wouldn't be a very successful reporter. I still don't know for sure who my father is. It still could be Ambrose."

"I meant no insult. You're bold enough to ask tough questions and persistent about it. Reminded me of a reporter. You could write stories, too. I know your mama educated you more'n was necessary. She didn't want you to wind up in a brothel." Mildred folded up the fabric, pins and all, and set it aside.

Estelle snorted. "If we move east, that may be the only thing I'm quali—" An older man entering the shop interrupted her dire self-critique.

"Howdy do, Miz Lowery. Just dropping my laundry for Miz Leona." He plopped a lumpy flour sack on Mildred's worktable. "I have this one shirt, well, Sarah had a mind to nibble the sleeve a bit." He pulled a blue plaid shirt out of the sack and laid the sleeve out flat. The elbow looked frayed and chewed. "It's got plenty of wear if'n I could just get a little patch here abouts."

Mildred pulled the shirt across the table and held up the offending sleeve. "Mr. Gentry, is this the same shirt I mended for you last month?" she snapped.

The man's cheeks flushed underneath his scraggly beard. "I think it's Sarah's favorite."

She inspected the other sleeve as well. "Humph. I'll patch both sleeves with suede and charge you extra. At least you'll be able to feel it before your mangy goat manages to chew through the leather."

"That's fine, that's fine, ma'am. I thank you." He looked back at the door then slid his gaze over Estelle before turning back to Mildred. "Now Miz Lowery, you know how I just hate gossip, don't listen to a bit of it?"

Mildred rolled her eyes and nodded as she crossed her arms. Estelle covered a smirk with her hand. This customer clearly enjoyed knowing what happened in town as much as the church ladies she'd met Sunday.

"Well, I did hear tell that you had a relation visitin'." His gaze darted to Estelle again and back to Mildred. "And I was wonderin' if she was related on your side or Mr. Lowery's."

She sighed. "What difference does it make, Mr. Gentry?"

"Well, the chatter is she don't *look* like someone from out east. Ain't that where your family is? That's where Miss Sarah, I mean Mizzus Taylor now, come from, ain't it? Didn't know you had more 'an one niece. I just want to set the record straight and stomp out any o' that vicious gossip. You know I don't truck with that."

"How is saying someone doesn't look eastern

considered vicious gossip?" Mildred asked.

The man leaned in over the table and lowered his voice. "The gossip is she runs with injuns. I don't want anyone to get the wrong idea about your kin. You're an upstanding lady. I want to correct any misunderstandins that I might happen to hear."

Mildred unfolded her arms and placed fisted hands on her hips. "Not that it is any of your business, Mr. Gentry, but Estelle and her brother Wabli are family friends, as dear to me as family. Wabli is half Lakota."

He straightened, sputtering. "I certainly didn't mean to offend." He turned to Estelle, finally removing his battered hat. "A pleasure to meet you Miz Estelle. I don't get to town but once a month or so. I hope you're enjoyin' your visit."

"I am, now. Your town is lovely, and it's been nice to catch up with my aunt." She smiled.

"Do you plan to stay long? I know of several beaus who might come callin'." He wiggled his bushy eyebrows, making Estelle laugh.

"Goodness. I don't know. Are you one of those beaus?"

Mildred snorted.

Mr. Gentry's jaw dropped. He clamped it shut and puffed out his chest. "I'm too old for you, sweetheart. You'll have to set your sights somewhere else. Your hair color has always been my favorite, but Sarah is the only girl for me. I'm too onery and set in my ways. Wouldn't dream of givin' up my bachelor lifestyle."

Estelle adopted a look of bitter regret. "That's a cryin' shame—"

Wabli burst into the shop from the back entrance. "Stella, come on! We need to go spring Thunder from the livery. He's going to think I left him."

"Wabli! You're being rude. This is a place of business. You can't charge in here like a, like a wild Indian," Mildred snapped.

Wabli's lips quirked as he suppressed a smile. "Yes, Auntie."

"No harm done, young man. I like to see a young person invested in his animal." Gentry gave Wabli a nod. "Did I hear you call this young lady Stella?" He turned back to Estelle. "That's a right purty name. Used to have a mule by that name." He clutched his hat to his chest. "Ol' Stella was my favorite, saw me through some tough times and helped ease a young man's bruised heart. Near broke me when she passed." He sighed and placed his hat back on his head. "But I have Sarah now, and she's waitin' for me at home. I'm gonna get on. I'll be back in a week or two to pick up my duds." He tipped his hat and left out the front door.

Shocked, Estelle turned to her aunt. "What was that man's name?"

Mildred returned her wide-eyed look and whispered, "That was Amos. Amos Gentry."

Estelle didn't need to ask after her aunt's ledgers after all. She was ready to go back to the Social Club.

****

Both Estelle's visit to the club and Wabli's liberation of Thunder were delayed by yet another summons, this time, to the jail. The Wild West Show had come to Wylder.

"There's my shooting star!" Miles Horton pointed finger guns at Estelle, blew on them, and stuffed them in his pockets. "And my ace racer." He wrapped an arm around Wabli's torso, being too short to meet her brother's shoulders, and mussed his hair. Wabli had been born while the show toured. Everyone considered him a beloved nephew…or pet of sorts.

"Miles, what are you doin' here?" Estelle asked.

"I learnt my three top attractions met with a spot of trouble. Figured I'd better come bail you out." He ran his hand down his dyed-black beard, playing the benevolent benefactor.

Estelle caught Sheriff Hanson's eye over Horton's shoulder and raised her eyebrows in question.

"Since Major Tucker put him in here," He jerked his chin at Ohan. "I sent for him to come sort it out."

Estelle nodded her thanks and surveyed the room before refocusing on her former boss. Two Indians sat in chairs against the wall. One read a dime novel and the other appeared to be asleep. Both wore full Indian leathers and headbands.

"Badger and Snake Hand came with me to collect you kids and Shadow Hawk." Horton was big on calling the Indians by the meanings of their Lakota names. If those names sounded foolish in English, Horton changed them to suit. In Ohanzee Cetan Wakuwa's case, Shadow Attacking Hawk was an oddly appropriate name for the man who'd cast such a big shadow on her life.

"I'm not going back," Wabli said.

"What he means is, it's time for both of us to part ways. Wabli is going to go to lawyer school and I'm going to go with him." Estelle tried to put it politely and gently. Horton had been good to her mother, a woman with a babe and nothing to recommend her but a pretty face and golden hair.

Horton chuckled. "You're goin' to lawyer school, too? Stella, I know you can ride and shoot as well or better than any man, but I think a fancy school would draw the line at letting you in." He shook his head at Wabli. "You either, kid, though I'm sorry as hell to have to say it. Come back with me, Stel. I'll write you a beautiful contract, better than your ma's since you ain't got dependents."

"Gilda." Ohan moaned forlornly from where he lay on his cell cot.

Estelle looked at the sheriff again.

Earl shrugged. "He wouldn't stop rantin' and ravin', but give him enough whisky and he passes out, nice and quiet. Heart broke and hungover's easier to listen to."

Ohan roused himself and staggered to the bars. "My son will come with me. He will sign a contract."

Wabli tensed, eyes wide with panic.

Chapter 22

Tucker hadn't been sure what to expect when he arrived at the jail. Ohan, still dressed in his fancy, though rumpled, suit stood at the cell bars yelling at Wabli with tears streaming down his face. Estelle argued with a short, balding man sporting a badly dyed beard and handlebar moustache. Sheriff Hanson leaned against the wall chatting with two Indians and Dooley sat in the corner of his cell shunning the entire assemblage.

The sheriff's relaxed demeanor told him there was no immediate danger to anyone and the situation could still be salvaged. But, where to start? He slammed the office door with more force than necessary. "What's going on here?"

Estelle turned. "Ohan's taking Wabli with him when he leaves."

The strange little man spoke. "Stella, Stella, you know we'll take good care of him. You, too. I don't know where you both got the ridiculous notion of him goin' to lawyer school, but darlin', it's just not possible." He really believed what he said. He spoke with pity rather than malice so Tucker wouldn't hate him—yet.

"He got the ridiculous notion from me. I'm going to sponsor him," Tucker said.

The man's gaze took in Tucker's uniform and skimmed over his shoulder boards. He thrust his hand out. "Miles Horton, Horton's Wild West Show. Whom do I have the privilege of addressin'?"

Tucker clasped Horton's hand firmly and shook. "I'm Major James Tucker. Wabli's been doing some work for me the last few weeks. He's quick, smart, and has a great deal of potential. He also has the heart and the determination to do something for the Lakota people, which will take him further than any of those other things."

"I know he's a good kid. I'd love to have him back, but it's not my call." He nodded his head at Ohan. "I'm just here to get my Indian. He's under contract. His little holiday's lasted long enough."

Tucker's gaze found Estelle. Her eyes pleaded with him. It seemed she trusted him, in this, at least. Wabli scooted over to stand by his sister when Tucker approached the bars. Ohan glared at him with bloodshot eyes.

"If you insist on taking Wabli with you, Estelle will press assault charges." At least Tucker hoped Estelle would agree to this plan. "Judge Read is still in town and can take care of it easily. I'm a witness, Chet Daniels witnessed the aftermath, and your own son can testify regarding a history of abuse." Without breaking eye contact he asked, "Sheriff, how long is an average sentence for assaulting a woman?"

"Well, if it were talking about simple stalking or harassment, you'd only be looking at a year. But when you up the charges to sexual assault in the second degrees it jumps to a minimum of five or as many as fifty."

Ohan blanched.

"Thank you, Sheriff. Your thorough knowledge of the legal system is appreciated."

"I like to keep up."

"What's it going to be, Ohan? You insist on taking Wabli, then Estelle presses charges and I get the pleasure of representing her against you before the judge. Or you walk away, and go back to your life at Horton's, Estelle drops the charges, and maybe one day your only son forgives you and tries to rebuild a relationship with you. Either way, you're not leaving here with that boy."

Ohan spit at Tucker's feet, the glob landing just shy of his boots. "Son will stay with sister."

Tucker turned back to the group. "I don't think we have any further business here. Sheriff, would you mind releasing the man after we've left?" The sheriff nodded affirmative. "Wabli, do you have anything else to say to your father?"

The boy looked at Ohan. "Thank you, Father. This is the best decision for me. I'll write." He brushed passed his sister as he fled out the door.

Horton turned to Estelle. "What about you, Stella? They may let the kid in with a fancy sponsor, but no fancy lawyer school is going to accept a girl. I can use your skills. You'll have your own sign." He formed an imaginary banner above his head with his hands. "Estrella the Shooting Star. See, we'd change your name up a little to make you more exotic, get you a sparkly gold costume like your mother's." The poor man didn't know Estelle at all if he thought any of those things would entice her back to that life.

Yet she seemed to hesitate.

"What else do you know how to do but ride and shoot?" Horton asked with sympathy.

The final comment seemed to solidify her resolve. "I'm sorry, Miles. That's not the life I want anymore and even if I did, I'd have to find another show to sign up with." Her gaze flicked to Ohan and Horton's followed it.

"All right, then. I wish you the best of luck, darlin'. You know how to find us if you change your mind." He stood on his toes and bussed her cheek.

"Thanks for everything, Miles." With barely a glance at Tucker, she followed her brother out of the building.

****

"You sent for me, Your Honor?" It was Saturday morning and Tucker had just finished releasing Captain Dooley to the military police soldier who'd arrived late the night before from Fort Laramie. A replacement would arrive to take over the cavalry office in Wylder the week after Thanksgiving.

Sheriff Hanson thanked them all for clearing the hell out of his jail and told Tucker the judge requested an audience.

"Come here, boy. Let me look at you. You certainly have the look of a Montgomery." The judge stared at him under bushy brows.

Tucker's eyes narrowed. "My name is Tucker, Your Honor, with all due respect."

Judge Read waved away his comment. "No matter. I wired your Colonel. Your mother's a Montgomery. Can't help she married an upstart." He shifted on the mattress mumbling under his breath. "New money whippersnapper."

"Be that as it may, did you need me for any particular reason or are we going to continue to discuss my relations?"

Read snorted. "Course I did. Here." He handed

151

Tucker an envelope that had been laying on the bedside table. "I had the attorney in town write this up for me, making things official. Pass me the whiskey. Fool woman left it out of my reach."

Tucker handed over the bottle and opened the envelope. He read it and re-read it. "What's the meaning of this?" he demanded.

"Just what it looks like. Congratulations, Honorable James Montgomery Tucker. As soon as I finish my drink, we can get on with the swearing-in bit." He tipped his head, allowing the amber liquid to flow into his mouth.

"I'm not qualified to be a circuit judge." Nor did he have any desire to be one.

Read set his empty glass on the table and held up a fist. He put up one stubby finger. "One, you're a lawyer." He added another finger with each point he made. "Two, you're a decorated cavalry officer. Three, you have a cousin in the senate and another in congress. Four, you're already here and familiar with the folk and their problems to a certain extent. Five, you have an uncle making a bid for the ding dang presidency. How much more qualified do you think you need to be to ride around the prairie deciding good from bad?"

"I need to think about this."

"Think all you want, but it's a done deal. This is an appointment, son, not a negotiation. Go ahead and raise your right hand."

Tucker numbly obliged. He placed his left hand on the Bible Read produced from underneath his pillow. None of Read's words penetrated the roaring in Tucker's ears of all his dreams slipping away.

Chapter 23

The last time Tucker got mad at her venturing off alone, Estelle ended up kissed against a wall in the livery. While thoroughly pleasant, she didn't want to listen to him fuss at her again, especially since his concerns proved to have some merit. Also, Wabli went and tattled on her, so Tucker was waiting downstairs when she left.

This was how Saturday morning, between the hours of ten and noon, she and the major came to have an audience with the lady of the house, Mrs. Adelaide Willowby.

"Won't you sit, Major?" The madam gestured to a wooden armchair tucked in the corner of the office.

"No, thank you. I prefer to stand, and I don't think we'll be here long." He took a sentry spot by the door.

Estelle settled into the same chair as before. Its squishiness had not improved any.

"Suit yourself. I'm glad you stopped in," Addie said, as if his presence there were pure happenstance. She circled the table and seated herself. "There has been a marked improvement in the behavior of our uniformed customers these last two weeks. I believe I owe you my thanks."

Tucker inclined his head. "I'm glad to hear it. The office will soon be under new management. That should forestall any future problems."

"Mmm. I did hear you were moving on soon."

After their last meeting, Estelle wasn't surprised the woman already knew about Tucker's appointment. She undoubtedly also knew the names Estelle had discovered, especially after the church debacle with Ezra and Widow Smithers.

As if reading her mind, Addie turned to Estelle. "Are you ready to tell me what you've discovered about the identity of your father?"

This was the moment of truth. Estelle felt the urge to wipe the smug expression from the madam's face. Her information network may be vast, but there was no way she could know about the clues revealed at her aunt's shop the day before. She took a deep breath before beginning. "I do. It's been a sad journey of discovery, and at times I regretted digging around in folks' pasts. My plan had been to ask you about Ambrose Barlow, though secrets came to light suggesting it couldn't possibly be him. No other candidates arose."

Mrs. Willowby nodded, sympathetic expression, real or false Estelle couldn't tell, etched on her face.

Estelle continued. "Until yesterday."

All sympathy fell away and one side of Addie's mouth twitched into a grin. "Indeed? So you have another name to put forth? You are correct, of course. Ambrose wasn't anyone's father. Besides, he never visited your mother."

Doubt rose in Estelle's chest. Addie said there were two possibilities. If Ambrose was never a contender, she was still short a possible father. "You said there were two names when I last saw you."

Tucker stepped behind her and placed his hand on her shoulder. His comforting presence steadied her resolve. No matter what she learned, or didn't learn, she'd put this behind her and move on. Her mother's mysterious *A* could remain a mystery. Nothing about her life would change.

"So, I did. Two men with *A* starting their first or last name visited the club during the prescribed time period. But only one of them visited your mother." She folded her hands serenely in her lap.

Estelle's ire spiked. She would have risen from her seat if not for Tucker's heavy hand. "You might have told me!"

"Where was the fun in that?" Her eyes sparkled with mirth. "If you thought you only searched for one man, you would have brought me Ambrose's name a week ago despite your misgivings. Come, now. Let's hear what you've discovered."

To Estelle's irritation, Addie was right. She'd continued to hope her aunt would come up with another name and planned to take a closer look at the cemetery. "Is Amos Gentry my father?"

Addie smiled in earnest. "Yes."

Tucker finally spoke. "How can you be certain? Surely there were numerous visitors during that time period."

"I won't take offense at your question, sir. You have no way of knowing how thorough my records are. Heavy snowfall during that time kept visitors away for the last two weeks of December 1953. Amos visited Amber just after the first of the year. Influenza had been making its rounds among the girls and Amber succumbed the following day and didn't receive anyone for two weeks. Farley closed the club through the end of January 1954 to ensure everyone returned to health. It could be no one but Amos."

Tucker squeezed her shoulder. "There's your answer. Are you pleased?"

She turned so she could look up at him. "I don't know yet if I'm pleased, exactly. Though I'm sorry for the trouble I caused them, I'm certainly *relieved* to not have to have anything more to do with Una and Ezra Barlow."

"I've no doubt there are a number of people in Wylder who wish they could say the same, myself included. Unfortunately, Ezra's money is as good as anyone else's, and he doesn't give us too much trouble anymore." Mrs. Willowby smirked, and her eyes twinkled. "If that's all, I really have a number of things to see to today."

She'd managed to get the information she came for from the infuriatingly secretive proprietress. She owed her at least a grudging thanks. She pasted her most pleasant smile on her face and rose as gracefully as possible from the chair. Tucker steadied her with a firm hand on her elbow. "Thank you so much for your assistance in this matter. I appreciate your time."

Addie's assessing gaze passed from Estelle to Tucker and back. Her grin deepened. "Good day, and good luck to you both."

****

They crossed back over the tracks and into town. Tucker would be leaving soon, and her life would be changing—somehow. Estelle may never have the opportunity to speak privately with him again. There were things that needed to be said.

She slowed her steps. "Tucker, James." His Christian name felt both foreign and intimate on her tongue. "I want to apologize for not telling you about

Ohan. You've been avoiding me, we've been avoiding each other, all week. I trust you more than anyone save my brother and I suppose, my aunt. I didn't want you to think me weak, and I didn't want you to look at me differently."

"All I wanted to do was protect you."

And love me? She dared hope.

"What Ohan did was something that happened to you. It didn't change who you are. I've had time to think on it and I understand. The apology is unnecessary, but since it has been burdening you, you're forgiven."

They'd stopped walking and faced each other. She longed for him to caress her cheek or touch her arm. How far she'd come from the first time they'd met. But he did neither of those things.

"We'll talk soon about what will happen with Wabli. It will be a little more challenging for me to organize since I'm stuck out here now." He leaned down a brushed his lips to her forehead. *Her forehead!* They resumed walking and stopped at the stairs to her door. "Good day, Estelle."

"Wait!" This couldn't be the end. Powerful attraction like theirs doesn't disappear. After everything they'd been through, it should be stronger than ever. It was for her. She'd witnessed new depths of Tucker's protective care of her. "Will you escort me tomorrow to see Amos?"

He nodded. "I'll be by in the morning."

Chapter 24

"This is farther out of town than I expected." Estelle glanced warily at the thickening forest. Even though they'd let the horses run part of the way, it still seemed to take a long time. Her anxiety about her objective might play a part, too.

"What did you expect with directions that read 'a far bit south of the river', 'twice as far as the lightening-struck tree', and 'on a ways after you take the left fork?'" Tucker asked.

"I'm just surprised. I couldn't see these trees from town."

"We're closer to the mountains; there's plenty of snowmelt to keep everything watered."

"Thank you for coming with me." It humbled her to admit she felt better having Tucker nearby.

"It was that, or deal with my anger later when I found out you took off to parts unknown by yourself." He slid his gaze to meet hers. "I know you can usually handle yourself, but even soldiers go out on patrol in pairs." He slowed Demon at a barely discernable gap in the trees. "I think this is it.

The overgrown path was just wide enough for a buckboard to pass through. Aunt Millie said Amos only came to town once a month or so now, and it showed. If he waited any longer between trips the forest might swallow him up.

Both Estelle and Tucker had to lean forward on their mounts to avoid low branches. Starlight pranced, unnerved by the dim light and unfamiliar surroundings. Demon side-stepped into her flank and snorted his irritation. Rude, but it served to settle the mare's rising anxiety. Estelle wished her own could be handled as easily.

They emerged from the trees into an open area. Open, except for a weathered clapboard house and innumerable ramshackle outbuildings. A yapping twisty-haired mutt ran out from behind the house prepared to tear into the intruders, provided it could be accomplished from thirty feet away.

Star shied and moved behind Demon, putting him between her and the perceived threat. Demon whinnied and stomped a foot, causing the guard to flee back to whence it came. No one noticed the man on the porch until the cocking of a rifle drew their attention.

"I hope you folks have a good reason for disturbin' my homestead and riling ol' Curley."

"Are you Amos Gentry?" Tucker asked in his authoritative officer voice.

Estelle slapped his arm and brought Starlight around so she could be seen from the porch. "Mr. Gentry, it's me, Estelle. We met at my aunt's dress shop a few days ago."

Amos squinted and lowered the rifle a fraction. "Miss Stella? If I'd a seen that hair first I would'a known right who it was." He raised the rifle again. "But I don't know this fella. Them soldiers in town are usually up to trouble. You shouldn't be consortin' with them."

Estelle smiled when Tucker grumbled under his breath. "This is Major Tucker," she called. "Both Sheriff

Hanson and my aunt vouched for him."

More yapping ensued. This time the mut, Curley, rounded the corner followed closely by a nanny goat. Amos finally set the rifle down and came ambling down the stairs.

"Dang it, Curley! Why'd you have to go bring Sarah into this? You know getting' excited puts her milk off. That's a whole pail for the hogs tonight." He grabbed the goat by the horns and pulled her to a stop just as Demon took a step back at this more formidable threat. Curley, for his part, plopped himself in the dirt by Amos's feet. "I apologize, Miss Stella. We don't get too many visitors. Shoo, Sarah, get on back to the barn." He slapped her on the hind quarters. She turned and bleated at him before trotting off. "That's what you always say!"

"Mr. Gentry, is there a place we can sit and talk? I want to talk about a relationship you—"

Amos turned beet red. "Now, Miss Stella, I done already told you I'm fixed in my bachelor ways. When I said I liked your hair I really wasn't flirtin' with ya. You're gonna have to set your sights on another beau."

Tucker's shoulders shook in silent laughter.

"Your relationship with my *mother*, Mr. Gentry. You knew her as Amber, your friend at the Social Club."

His eyebrows rose and studied Estelle hesitantly. "I think maybe you and soldier boy here better come in. You can tie your horses at the trough, yonder." He walked back toward the house as if he'd aged ten years in the last ten minutes.

****

"Got no sugar. Can't abide it." Amos set mismatched tin cups of coffee in front of Estelle and Tucker.

160

"I don't take sugar, either." She glanced at Tucker who took a sip but couldn't quite hide his grimace.

"I'm fine." He held up is cup. "I like a good stout brew."

Amos settled onto a stool across from Estelle and wrapped his hands around his own mug. "Good, good. I'm glad there was still enough left in the pot from yesterday mornin'."

Estelle bit back a smile as Tucker quickly lowered his cup just before another swallow of liquid touched his lips.

"I'm not a clever man, but I can add two and two. Amber's passed on, hasn't she."

Unexpected tears filled Estelle's eyes as she nodded. "Cancer. A few months ago."

Amos blinked back his own tears. "She mention me?"

"No, but she kept a journal. I suspect you're the mysterious *A* she wrote of so fondly. The person she was certain fathered me."

A lone tear trickled down Amos's wrinkled face and disappeared into his wiry mustache. He snuffled, staring down at the tabletop. "I wanted to propose and take her outa that place. I didn't come back to town for a couple months, busy with plantin' and such. When I came back to town, she weren't at the club no more. I was too embarrassed and too proud to ask after her. I figured she didn't feel the same as me and got a better offer. I'm a fool."

"She knew you had a good reputation. She didn't want you to marry her and risk the ridicule of the town. She didn't want it for you, and she didn't want it for me. I don't agree. She loved you very much, Amos. I think you would have made each other happy." Estelle wrapped her hand around his.

Amos finally met her gaze, tears flowing steadily now. "She named you after my favorite mule."

Estelle nodded. "I figured that out when you mentioned it the other day. I went to see Mrs. Willowby to confirm it." Something clicked. "My mother *did* tell stories about you. She called you the animal talker. She made up all kinds of funny stories." Though, now having met the man, she wondered if some of them were true.

He wiped his nose and chuckled. "I talked to her about Stella, my mule. Had a different dog then, too. Ol' Bill." His face grew solemn. "I never went back, you know, to the Social Club. I couldn't bear bein' there without her. Couldn't bear the thought of bein' with anyone else." He reddened and ducked his head. "I ain't never had a daughter."

"I've never had a father, either. We'll figure it out as we go."

****

Tucker forced Demon to walk most of the way back to town. Estelle didn't say much but seemed at peace. He thought about poor Amos, living alone in his regret the past twenty-four years and couldn't imagine a more pitiful existence.

He'd never considered himself a prideful man. He'd shared kisses and touches with Estelle like he might a woman he courted. Scratch that. He never would have behaved so inappropriately with a society Miss. It shamed him that he hadn't had the discipline to treat Estelle with the same respect.

She challenged him and fired his blood. She was fiercely independent yet brought out his protective instincts. So ignorant in his own hubris, he never considered the perfect Boston ladies he thought he wanted, weren't what he needed. He wasn't the same man anymore and hadn't been for a long time.

For all his dislike of the west, the east wouldn't suit him anymore either, like trying to put on a coat he'd long outgrew. He'd grown and changed. His desire for Estelle, for the wildness of her, was a reflection of that growth. He wouldn't make the same mistakes as Amos. He wouldn't be the fool who let her go.

****

Estelle waited while Tucker tied Demon to the rail again, this time with firm admonishments and threats, then followed her into the livery. He helped her make quick work of grooming and feeding Star. She could tell something plagued him. He'd tell her eventually. He had a hard time keeping his opinions to himself when it came to her.

"We need to talk."

"We are talkin'." She lifted her saddlebag over her shoulder, preparing to leave. She didn't know if she wanted to hear whatever he'd been mulling over for so long. "Thank you for coming with me."

"Wait." He took the bag from her and hung it on a hook next to his hat, then turned and took her hand in his. "I haven't done right by you, haven't treated you properly. I want you to come with me, on the circuit, be my wife."

Her heart sped up, could he still have feelings for her, too?

"I've taken liberties usually only allowed a man who's made a declaration, and I want to remedy that."

Estelle yanked her hand from his. "I won't leg

163

shackle myself to you because you feel guilty. This isn't old England where we'd have to marry because I'm compromised by being alone with you. You can go hang yourself and your fancy morals."

Tucker raked a hand through his hair. "This isn't coming out correctly." He captured her hand again. "Estelle, you have driven me to the brink of insanity from wanting you. You challenge me at every turn, yet I've never felt more alive than I do when I'm with you. It's as if I've awoken from a long sleep into the beginning of a dream. "

It shocked her to hear the feelings pour out of this staid, buttoned-up man.

"When I say that I haven't respected you, what I mean is that it took me too long to realize how important you are to me. I'm ashamed of my loss of control. I want to make it right, not out of guilt, though I do feel guilty, but because I don't want to risk losing you. Visiting Amos helped me put a lot of things into perspective. Come with me."

As he spoke, Estelle thought about the things she'd done. She trusted Tucker more than any other man she'd ever known. It made her careless with her heart and in her actions. He claimed he'd taken liberties, well she'd more than encouraged them. Could she trust him with her future? He'd proven himself thus far with their dealings and his defense of Wabli.

"What about Wabli? If you're sending him to school, I want to be where he is. He doesn't have anyone else."

"He can put off school for a year or so and travel with us. He can apprentice under me during that time. In the long run, that experience will put him ahead of his peers and hopefully open doors that would otherwise be closed due to his Lakota roots. If he agrees, will you? Will you be my wife?"

"I'm not going to change. I'm going to ride and carry a gun and wear trousers. I'm not saying I'll never wear a skirt, but you've got to know up front, this is me." She held his gaze, praying it wouldn't be too big a stumbling block.

He never blinked. "If you changed, you wouldn't be the woman I've come to admire, to love."

She smiled. "Look at me, I'm collecting male relations left and right today. A father this morning and a husband this afternoon."

He smiled and his body relaxed in evident relief. Estelle hadn't realized how tense he'd been holding himself. "A fiancé this afternoon," he corrected. "It might be too late in the day to pull together a wedding. But I can probably make it happen in a day or two before Judge Read leaves town."

"I'd like that. Are we done talkin'?" She really hoped they were.

He leaned in, fire alight in his eyes, and proved talking was overrated until Demon demanded his attention.

Epilogue

"I don't care what anyone else says about it, Widder Lowrey, you are a mighty fine cook. You prolly could have done wonders with them skinny squirrels I offered up." Amos complimented his hostess in between bites.

"Thank you, Mr. Gentry. I thought the grouse my niece and her husband shot were more appropriate for my Thanksgiving table, but I do appreciate the offer," Mildred replied.

Estelle couldn't remember when she'd last felt so content, maybe never. Her makeshift family crowded around the table at the Taylor ranch. Aunt Millie and her true niece, Sarah, prepared the grouse she and Tucker had lucked upon when he'd taken her target shooting. The table sagged with dishes of potatoes, bread, squash, nuts, and pumpkin pie.

In barely a week, she, Tucker, and Wabli would begin Tucker's circuit route. He would be, officially, a Mister now instead of a Major, though technically, she supposed he would be addressed as Honorable. She had been Mrs. James Tucker for less than a week and had loved every minute of it. Her face heated as she thought of her favorite moments in particular.

Tucker raised his glass. He'd been so excited to find a bottle of cranberry wine from a familiar New England winery. It complimented the meal perfectly. "I'd like to propose a toast to our host and hostess, Daniel and Sarah

Taylor."

"Here, here!" everyone said, glasses raised.

Tucker wasn't finished. "Today is a day set aside for being thankful. I know everyone at this table has something to be thankful for. I'm happy to be moving forward with my wife and my new brother-in-law and to know that no matter where we go, we'll have family here in Wylder to welcome us when we come back."

Amos stumbled to his feet. "I never had a thought about walking a daughter down the aisle and now it's the best day of my life. Though I'm not a bit happy about giving my only daughter away less than a week after I got her." He tried to scowl at Tucker, but a goofy grin broke through instead.

Everyone shared around the table and finally it was Estelle's turn. "Most everything you all said are the same things I'm thankful for, too. The only thing I can add is this, I'm thankful for my mother. She went through the worst time of her life here in Wylder. Despite that, she found love and friendship strong enough to draw me back to this place, where I've now found love, friendship, and so much more." She glanced at Tucker, Aunt Millie, and finally Amos, then raised her glass. "To Gilda, may she rest in Glory."

"To Gilda."

A word about the author...

Shelley is a twenty-five year resident of Oklahoma with roots in Maine. She and her husband have four awesome kids, but are thrilled two have successfully reached adulthood and moved out. She spends her time working with students, writing, reading, baking, sewing, and exercising just enough to counteract her other activities. Too Wyld for Comfort is her second Wylder tale.

Thank you for purchasing
this publication of The Wild Rose Press, Inc.

For questions or more information
contact us at
info@thewildrosepress.com.

The Wild Rose Press, Inc.
www.thewildrosepress.com

www.ingramcontent.com/pod-product-compliance
Lightning Source LLC
Chambersburg PA
CBHW060114260626
47160CB00005B/1887